COVERED BRIDGE

Other books by Brian Doyle

Covered Bridge

BRIAN DOYLE

A Groundwood Book
Douglas & McIntyre
TORONTO / VANCOUVER / BUFFALO

Groundwood Books/Douglas & McIntyre Ltd.
585 Bloor Street West
Toronto, Ontario M6G 1K5

The publisher gratefully acknowledges the assistance of
the Ontario Arts Council and the Canada Council.

Canadian Cataloguing in Publication Data

Doyle, Brian
    Covered bridge

ISBN 0-88899-190-8

I. Title.

PS8557.O95C68   1993   jC813'.54   C93-094333-3
PZ7.D79Co   1993

Map by Megan Doyle
Design by Michael Solomon
Cover art by Paul Zwolak
Printed and bound in Canada

Thanks Patsy Aldana, Fay Beale,
Stan Clark, Keith Clarke, Jackie Doyle,
Megan Doyle, Mike Doyle, Ryan Doyle,
Paul Kavanagh, Marilyn Kennedy,
Dorothy McConnery, Cathy McGregor,
Mike Paradis, Dr. Peter Premachuk,
Rita Premachuk, Gene Rheaume,
and Alan Wotherspoon,
for your expertise and support.

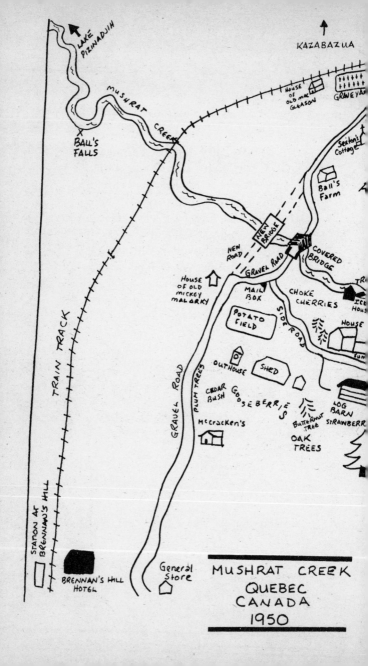

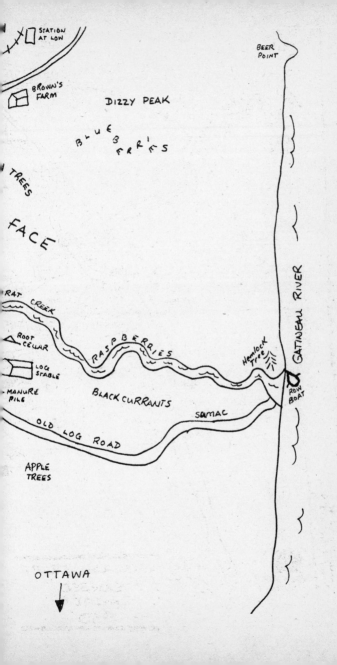

CRICKETS ACTUALLY
ARGUE!

My dog Nerves and I stood in the almost dark inside the portal of the covered bridge. My eyes were squinting, trying to see what was coming slowly, floating through the bridge towards us from the other end. I could feel one of Nerves' knees knocking against the side of my shoe.

The moon put a patch of silver-yellow through the open wind space in the lattice onto the deck about halfway between us and the white thing gliding towards us. The rafters above were off in the dark. The carriageway under our feet was dark except for the patch of moon.

Mushrat Creek burbled and gurgled quietly under us. Nerves' teeth were grinding and chattering politely beside my ankle.

Somewhere else, two crickets were arguing.

The thing took more shape as it approached the wind space. The shape of a woman. And a voice, saying words.

"Please, father, let me in? Please let me in, father! May I please go in? Can't I please get in?"

She wore a moonlight-coloured dress and a wide-brimmed dark hat.

There was no face showing under the hat.

Nerves stopped knocking and went stiff against me.

Then the woman turned in the moonlight and hurtled through the space and disappeared into Mushrat Creek.

Then we heard a big splash.

That is, I heard a big splash.

Nerves didn't hear a thing.

He was passed out.

That was the first night of my new job on the covered bridge.

The next day I was fired.

But we're going too fast.

I'd better go back a bit.

CHIPWAGON BECOMES
U.F.O.!

You probably heard about how my father was run over by a streetcar. How he lay down on the streetcar tracks for a rest during a snowstorm. I never knew him because that happened when I was just a baby.

My mom died when I was born. I lived with Mrs. O'Driscoll. She was married to a distant cousin of my dad's. I thought of her as my mother and I loved her. But I called her Mrs. O'Driscoll. It was a warm little joke we had between us.

And you probably heard about all that stuff that happened to me at Glebe Collegiate and at the Uplands Emergency Shelter where we lived and about Easy Avenue and my job with Miss Collar-Cuff and the mysterious money and about Mr. Donald D. DonaldmcDonald and about O'Driscoll showing up from the War almost five years late.

And about the fight I had with Fleurette Featherstone Fitchell and how we made up after and went on a picnic with everybody.

But I definitely didn't yet tell how I wound up on a little farm up the Gatineau at Mushrat Creek in charge of a covered bridge and what happened about the bridge.

But before any of *that* happened I guess I didn't tell you how Fleurette Featherstone Fitchell moved away in the middle of the night one night, and the next morning there was nothing left of her except a short note to me pinned to our door. It was in a sealed envelope.

The note said this:

Dear Hubbo:
My Dear Hubbo:

I will always, all my life, love you.
Dad is back and we're leaving now.
Right now.
Everything is going to be better from now on, he said.

xxxxx in the middle of the night.
F[3]

And I also didn't tell you about how I couldn't write her back because she didn't tell anybody where she was going. I asked all the neighbours if they knew, I asked the post office across the parade square, I phoned the office where we paid our rent. Nobody knew what Featherstone Fitchell's new address was. They were just gone. Vanished. Fleurette, into thin air.

There was so much I wanted to tell her, to talk to her about.

I started a letter to her that I couldn't send. Not now, anyway. But you never know. She might show up. O'Driscoll, he was supposed to be drowned, dead, vanished in the War, and he came back. So maybe I would find her address or maybe she would get in touch with us sometime. I guess, then, it was because of the miracle of O'Driscoll showing up that I started the letter to Fleurette.

I told her that I couldn't send it, which seemed to be a pretty stupid thing to say, because, if I couldn't send it, she wouldn't hear me say that, and if I could send it, I wouldn't have to say what I just said.

Then I asked her if she remembered that afternoon we had the picnic at the sand pits and how O'Driscoll came down the hill of sand and how he stopped in front of us? And how he took a look back over his shoulder? And how, then, he spoke? And, after nine years away, what was the first thing he said?

"Well, now," says O'Driscoll, "what were we talking about before this interruption? Where were we, anyway?"

Then I reminded her, in the letter, how Mrs. O'Driscoll never said a word, just took a step forward, stomping on her sherry glass lying in the sand, and fell against his chest and put her cheek on his shoulder and her nose in his neck and her arms around him, and closed her eyes, squeezed her eyes shut.

But O'Driscoll's eyes weren't shut. He was looking at me. I remembered him from his picture, not from real life.

"You're young Hubbo," he said over the top of Mrs. O'Driscoll's head. That made me feel good. He made me feel like he'd be disappointed if I wasn't young Hubbo. O'Driscoll was like that. He could make you feel good.

Then I told Fleurette all about O'Driscoll and the chipwagon. And how, after we'd had the wagon only three days, something awful happened. We were crossing the train tracks that crossed Ottawa along Scott Street. Right on the tracks, a wheel fell off our wagon. We got the horse unhitched just in time.

The Scott Street line is pretty straight so we had time to unbuckle the traces and get the horse out of the shafts. The train didn't even try to slow down at the last minute. It was in the morning and the train was coming in from the west so I guess the sun was in the engineer's eyes. At least that's what they said afterwards.

O'Driscoll said he thought they did it on purpose. He said he heard the old engineer saying to the fireman that he'd hit a lot of things in his long career — cows, buffalo, a truck full of turkeys, a tramp who'd frozen to death, a house on a trailer — but never a chipwagon, and he was glad he did because he always wanted to see what it was like. See how high the wagon would go.

He wasn't disappointed.

O'Driscoll said that it was probably the best hit that engineer ever had in his long years as a rotten train driver. The air was full of potato chips and paper plates and toothpicks for about a half an hour. It poured salt.

And it rained grease.

The main part of the wagon turned over and over in the air and the unpeeled potatoes were flying and bouncing around like hail the size of baseballs.

I told Fleurette some other stuff about O'Driscoll's insurance and how he put a down payment on a little farm up here in a place called Mushrat Creek. Then I told her about how the dog, Nerves, was ours now because his family didn't want him anymore.

Then I wrote a letter to the Uplands Emergency Shelter post office.

Dear Sir:

Please send me the address of Fleurette Feather-stone Fitchell who moved out of Building Number Eight, Unit 3 at the end of June, 1950.

We don't know where she went.

Yours truly,

Hubbo O'Driscoll

P.S. My new address is:
Hubbo O'Driscoll,
Mushrat Creek,
c/o Brennan's Hill Post Office,
Gatineau County,
Quebec, Canada.

FISH JUMPS OUT
OF FRYING PAN!

From my bedroom window I could hear the fish jumping in Mushrat Creek. You can't *hear* fish jumping, but you can hear the water take a double kind of a slurp. Sometimes the two slurps happen so fast together it sounds like only *one* nice delicious slurp. But it's really two. One when the trout comes out of the water with his mouth open and his gills stretched to get the bug he's after, and the other for when he flips his body and his tail hits the top of the water to get him back down into Mushrat Creek.

I suppose he thinks he's safe down there but you'd think he'd know everybody can see where he's going and what he's doing because the water's so clear you can see right to the bottom. But I guess he does know because he likes to take his bug or his caterpillar or his fly or whatever he's caught and swim with it under the overhanging alders or beneath where the grassy bank juts out or into the weeds or under the wharf out of the light.

He's probably like everybody else. You go where it's dark, where it's private, then nobody can see you. You *think*.

It's like the covered bridge.

Sometimes people go in there to do things that they don't want anybody to see them doing because it's dark in there at certain times of the day and night and it seems private.

But you never know who might be watching.

It wasn't these thoughts, though, that woke me up that morning.

It was the sounds of the trout jumping in Mushrat Creek.

And our rooster crowing.

I got up and lit a small hot fire in the stove in the summer kitchen and put on a kettle of well-water. I put a dipper of creek water from the pail into the basin and washed up.

I stepped outside to dry my face.

The sun was already giving the white trunks of the birch trees across Mushrat Creek and up on the top of Rock Face a bit of a golden glow. Upstream, though, to the west, the red side of the covered bridge was still a grey shadow. And west of that, up at Ball's Falls and Lake Pizinadjih, it would still be dark.

It was O'Driscoll who told me how to watch a sunrise. He learned it when he was a sailor in the war. He said you watch not the sun where it is supposed to come up, but something else.

Watch the flag away above you on the ship to get the first flash of light. Because the flag is higher than you, it will see the sun first. Specially when the sea is calm.

So he told me to watch the white birch trees standing on the top of Rock Face across Mushrat Creek, because they'd get the sun before I would see it. Or, even better, watch Dizzy Peak to the north, if it was clear.

This morning I missed it.

But that was O.K. because the next flash of light would be on the covered bridge and the tops of the trees, which were both higher than our house.

The rooster gave another couple of crows because he was watching for the light too.

I went down the short hill and cut through the ice house and stepped out on the little wharf on Mushrat Creek. My fishing rod was lying right where I left it in the cattails beside the wharf.

I baited my hook with a small worm I got out of my worm can that I kept in the ice house between two blocks of ice to keep cool. Worms like the cool. They might as well be nice and cool and have a nice life for a while because what was going to happen to them pretty soon wasn't nice at all.

Three worms — three brook trout. I pulled three brook trout from where they were hiding. The worms helped me. Fish eat worms. The O'Driscolls eat fish. That's Nature!

I cut open the stomachs and left the heads on and cleaned the bodies slippery clean in the clear water of Mushrat Creek.

I took them through the ice house and up the short hill to the summer kitchen attached to the back of our house.

I liked to cut through the ice house whenever I had the chance. Because of the smell of the damp sawdust and the wooden floor and the cold smell of the ice mixed with the wood and the log walls and the oakum stuffed between the logs.

It reminded me of jumping on the backs of the ice wagons to grab an ice chip to chew on a hot August day in Lowertown when I lived there and was small.

In the summer kitchen I put an iron frying pan on the stove, got a slab of butter from the ice box, some flour out of the bin. I melted the butter in the pan,

18

rolled the trout in the flour and placed them carefully in the sizzling butter.

One of the trout bodies twitched a bit. Jumped.

"Now that's fresh fish," O'Driscoll would say.

I cut two slabs of bread and clamped them in the wire toaster. I lifted one of the stove lids. I put on the toast. I turned over the trout. I poured the boiling water over the tea bags in the pot. I turned the toast.

I moved the trout a bit in the pan. No more jumping. Getting brown in the hot butter.

I shook the fire. I made other breakfast noises. I knew that upstairs they would like to hear the breakfast noises.

I turned the toast again and then took it off and plastered both pieces with homemade butter. I put the lid back on the hole and placed the toast on the rack to keep warm.

Then I called upstairs.

The first of the family to come downstairs was Nerves.

I told you about Nerves, who we got from our neighbour at Uplands Emergency Shelter when we lived there. Nerves was our little dog who looked a lot like a rat. His tail was a little black whip, and he clicked when he walked. This morning his little eraser of a nose was moving around, smelling breakfast. Then he yawned and stretched and went to the door. While he was waiting for me to shove open the screen door for him (he usually opened it himself but this morning he was too tired), he leaned his little head on the doorjamb and closed his eyes. Seeing the ghost had played him right out.

I let Nerves out and heard the stairs creak.

After breakfast I would tell them about what Nerves and I saw last night.

FARMERS FALL OFF
EDGE OF EARTH!

We sat down to breakfast and Mrs. O'Driscoll's eyes were shining. She loved this farm. She felt like she lived on it all her life and it was only our second week there.

The people before us, the what's-their-names, had kept it up pretty well, but there was still lots to do. The people before us were only leasing it to us while they went on a world tour that they won. They won it in a baking contest. Something they baked.

They would be back in a year.

Maybe. Who knows.

Look how long it took O'Driscoll to come back!

And Mrs. O'Driscoll got to work right away as soon as we got there. Before O'Driscoll was even unpacked, Mrs. O'Driscoll had filled a half a pail with gooseberries she picked out near the cedar trees behind the outhouse. And the next day she had six jars of gooseberry jam sitting down in a neat row in the cool root cellar behind the henhouse.

I never saw Mrs. O'Driscoll work so hard and be so happy. Jam and pie and jelly and cake and homemade bread; washing, ironing, sewing, weeding, milking, separating, churning, scrubbing, feeding, picking, singing and laughing.

And O'Driscoll and I were busy, too; cutting and carrying and chasing and fixing, and hoeing and harnessing, and shingling and wiring and talking...talking...

O'Driscoll was talking.

"Did you know that the first covered bridge ever built on this planet was over the Euphrates River in the year 783 Before Christ? And that bridge is still there? At least I think it's still there. I'm not sure if I saw it or not or maybe I'm imagining it because of the amnesia. Or I saw a drawing of it somewhere," O'Driscoll was saying as he finished up his trout breakfast.

"The Euphrates River is in Egypt somewhere, O'Driscoll. How could you get to Egypt if you were in the South Pacific?" Mrs. O'Driscoll asked. She didn't seem to care if she got an answer. She was too happy to bother with answers. She always liked questions better than answers.

"Amnesia is a peculiar thing," O'Driscoll said. "You never know whether what you say about yourself is true or what. Like that business about prospecting for uranium in Labrador. I was sure about that, but now it doesn't seem real."

"Well, O'Driscoll," said Mrs. O'Driscoll, "don't bother your head about it. You're here now. We're all three of us here now and that's all that counts. We'll just prove to the government you're not dead and you can get your veteran's money and it'll all be forgotten."

"And the *longest* covered bridge in the world is right here in Canada. It's in New Brunswick and it's over the Saint John River. It's 1,282 feet long. And it's there as large as life because I was there and I saw it with these two eyes. I remember that as well as I remember this beautiful trout breakfast you made for us this morning, Hubbo me boy!"

O'Driscoll was never the kind of person who didn't listen to what you were saying. That is, most of the time. But when it came to something that might be a little bit unbelievable, he might not listen very well. Maybe he'd think you were exaggerating a little bit. I wondered where he'd ever get an idea like that.

"Nerves and I went down to look over the job after dark. Didn't get anything done. Saw a ghost..."

"A ghost, eh?" said O'Driscoll. "Well, those old bridges are full of ghosts... anyway, if you do well your first month or so, you'll be full-time caretaker at least until the what's-their-names come back. We could use the $12 a month..."

"It was the shape of a woman ... it jumped into the creek... Nerves passed out... I was saying..." But O'Driscoll kept talking.

"Your job is to keep the lights in shape, report any damage or accidents or suspicious happenings and oversee the painting of the bridge every two years. The two years is coming up a month or so from now. There's expenses. Oil, wicks, tools and, of course, the paint and the labour during paintin' time is what the expenses are for."

"There was a splash. She had on a whitish dress and a dark hat with big brim," I said quietly.

O'Driscoll was looking at me with pride.

I was saying just the kind of things that he would say. When I mentioned the splash, Mrs. O'Driscoll put her hands across the table, one on mine and one on O'Driscoll's, and smiled.

Then she said this out of the far corner of her

mouth: "I love it here. Ghosts and covered bridges and everything! Are we ever *lucky*! I hope that the what's-their-names fall of the edge of the earth on that world tour of theirs and that they're never heard from again."

"I'll drink to that," said O'Driscoll, and gulped down the rest of his tea. They weren't going to listen to me about the ghost.

I was starting to think that maybe it never happened.

If only Nerves could talk. He didn't think it was so *lucky*!

A knock came to our front door. I went through the parlour we only used on Sunday and opened the front door we hardly *ever* used. It was stuck and I had to give it an extra shove and a kick.

It was the county chairman.

In our kitchen, he told us we didn't need to caretake the covered bridge anymore. We were getting a new bridge. I was fired.

It was the shortest job I ever had.

BOOK CAUSES
EARTHQUAKE!

O' Driscoll was talking about the construction going to start about a mile up Mushrat Creek. They were going to build a modern bridge over the creek so the highway would go straight through instead of circling down to the covered bridge like it always did. This would take a big bend out of the road.

He also said a couple of times that he heard some of the farmers up in the post office in Low talking about the highway getting paved.

"That'll keep the dust off the chokecherries begod!" O'Driscoll told us one of them said.

And everybody was saying how good it was going to be because there would be jobs for everybody that wanted to work and there'd be money galore around for everybody.

And O'Driscoll explained once while we were milking the cows that the farmers around there had a pretty good life even though they had to work pretty hard for it.

But the one thing they never had very much of was money.

All the money they ever had was from the cream

they sold to the dairy or maybe they'd sell a pig or a steer or maybe even raise some chickens and sell them but not very often.

And once when we were in the general store in Brennan's Hill buying what we needed which was salt, flour, tea, sugar and molasses, we heard the owner of the store say that his hired man quit on him to go and work on the new highway that was to approach the new bridge.

We bought more molasses than other people, mostly because it was our dog Nerves' favourite food.

Nerves loved to eat a big chunk of bread soaked in molasses.

What a dog.

Then he'd go down to the creek and wash his hands and face.

Maybe take a swim.

One hot afternoon Mrs. O'Driscoll was sitting in her rocking chair out the front doorway in the shade of her two rowanwood trees. She looked nice rocking there a little bit in her bright yellow and blue dress and the purple combs in her hair and above her the clumps of red rowanwood berries hanging like tiny chandeliers. And her head resting back and a little smile on her face. She liked that yellow and blue dress because yellow and blue were the school colours of the school, Glebe Collegiate, where she worked as a cleaning lady before she became a farmer.

She had on the stove a great big pot of preserves simmering away in the summer kitchen.

The smell of the raspberries bubbling there in the sugary red syrup was reaching out through the screen door, past the woodpile, over the side road, around the walls of the barn and into the pig pen

25

where the pigs were lying in the cool mud in the hot sun grunting and snorting and sighing every now and then and snuffling into their big nostrils the sweetness and the pureness of Mrs. O'Driscoll's great big pot of preserves of raspberries simmering on the stove in her summer kitchen.

And upstairs, in the heat, the way O'Driscoll liked it (Mrs. O'Driscoll said out of the corner of her mouth he must have been in the North Pole all the time he was away and he's trying to make up for it now), O'Driscoll lay sleeping, grunting and snorting a little bit and breathing in the hot raspberry syrupy smell that floated into the house from the summer kitchen up through the vent in the ceiling and right around O'Driscoll's body and up around his head.

I went down to the ice house and sat in there on an old car seat in the cool corner in the sawdust. The smell of the oakum between the logs was almost like chloroform, and I dozed off a bit and let my book, *War and Peace*, fall to the floor.

The noise the book made when it hit the floor shook the whole building.

And the ground.

It was deep noise, a thud from the centre of the earth.

No, it wasn't the book! A book couldn't do that! I was awake now.

It was dynamite!

They were blasting about a mile up Mushrat Creek.

Construction for the new bridge was starting.

A while later, some dead trout floated by. They floated on their backs, their white stomachs shining in the sun, the dark pink of the inside of their gills like little ribbons around their necks.

GOOSEBERRY HAS FACE
OF A BEAUTIFUL WOMAN!

I was writing more stuff to Fleurette. Trying to explain about Mrs. O'Driscoll and how happy she seemed to be. Her face, it was, it looked, it seemed like she was just going to start smiling any minute now. How some people's faces look like they are just about to start crying and other people's faces look like they are just going to get mad and start shouting at somebody.

But Mrs. O'Driscoll, her face was so different from what it used to be like. When she was a cleaning lady at Glebe Collegiate Institute and we lived at Uplands Emergency Shelter her face was often like one of those faces that might start to sigh any minute or maybe even start to cry.

And I tried to tell Fleurette how maybe it was because O'Driscoll was lost in the war and how it was only when she had some of the sherry that she liked that she wore her face in a different way.

But now, here at Mushrat Creek with O'Driscoll, Mrs. O'Driscoll's face was the same whether she had the sherry or not.

And I tried to think of what to compare Mrs. O'Driscoll's face to, to put in Fleurette's letter.

Her face was calm like the covered bridge. It was content like Mushrat Creek. It was clear like Dizzy Peak. It was funny like a gooseberry on a gooseberry bush. And it was full of love like the Gatineau Hills.

And it was wise, like the Gatineau River.

Fleurette would like these ways that I tried to say what Mrs. O'Driscoll's face was like.

And I was writing how you get to like somebody's face. Like O'Driscoll's. At first I thought he was sort of funny-looking. Now I loved his face. What happened? It didn't look like the same face at all.

But mostly I was trying to explain how they were going to let the bridge get old and rotten. How you have to take care of things or they'll disappear.

Or maybe they would just let it get neglected until it got dangerous, and then they'd have to tear it down.

It didn't seem right.

Mailman Enters
Covered Bridge –
Does Not Exit!

T he very first person I met around Mushrat
Creek was Oscar McCracken.

Oscar McCracken's farm was the last farm
on the road going south before you got into Brennan's Hill.

Oscar lived there with his mother and his younger
brother. He worked hard on the farm and also delivered the mail twice a day in his little car with only
a front seat.

It was a pretty old car. A 1929 Ford Coupe. You
could open the windshield by winding a handle on
the dashboard. You cranked the motor with a hand
crank to start it. It had two narrow steps under each
door called running boards.

The train came up in the evening and went down
in the morning. Oscar met the train at ten to six in
the evening in Brennan's Hill and picked up the mail
and delivered it up along the road past our place as
far as Low.

Then he drove back home.

He also met the train in the morning at ten after
nine in Low and did his route again.

That meant he crossed the covered bridge four times a day.

About a week after we moved in I walked down our side road past the potato field on one side and the dusty chokecherry trees on the other side to our gate at the main gravel road and our mailbox. The entrance to the covered bridge was right there on the right.

I stood leaning on the gate because I wanted to find out something. I wanted to find out why it took so long for the mail car to go through the bridge. First you'd hear it stop at the house of Old Mickey Malarkey and you'd hear the mail box squeak and the car door slam. Then you'd hear the car groan in first gear, hear it swallow, hear it whine in second gear, hear it swallow and just hear it start crying in third gear and then stop in front of our mailbox. After the mailman put in our mail (it was never for us at first, it was always for the farmers who were going to fall off the edge of the earth), you could hear the car door slam, the motor moan in first gear, swallow, whine in second gear...but then the car would be inside the bridge and you wouldn't be able to hear as well, except for the rumbling of the wheels on the carriageway...then silence.

Sometimes two or three minutes would pass by before you would hear even any rumbling and then the car would burst out the other side, whining in second gear.

You could hear the thunk of the ramp as the wheels left the deck. Then, swallow, high gear and gone.

I stood there leaning on our gate to see if I could see why it took the mailman so long to get through the covered bridge.

Along he came to Malarkey's. I followed him with my ears:

squeak (the mail box),

slam (the car door),

first gear, groan, swallow (gearshift), second gear, whine,

swallow, third gear, cry...stop.

The mailman got out. He came over to me and told me his name. Oscar McCracken. He gave me a catalogue. He got back in the car. He drove into the covered bridge and stopped about half the way in. He shut off the motor. He sat there.

I could feel the silence he was in as I leaned over our gate to get a better look.

After a long while, Oscar McCracken got out, cranked his car started, got back in and drove out the other side of the bridge and up the road towards Low.

I walked into the bridge and stopped almost half-way over and waited. I listened to Mushrat Creek below and to the swallows twittering secretly in the mud nests in the rafters. I was standing beside the gap in the siding which was for air circulation and also for cutting down on wind obstruction.

And for letting in the moon some nights. And for ghosts to dive out of.

Up in the rafters near the eaves was a gap, left there also for circulation and wind.

Further up the rafters closer to the arch, near where the end of a tree-knee angle brace met on one of them, there was something written. Carved in the wood.

I crawled partway up the truss using the ventilation gaps and the timbers and braces for my hands and feet until I could make out the writing.

31

The catalogue I still had in my hand slipped between my fingers, bounced off my foot and through the gap and down into Mushrat Creek.

I didn't even know I had it in my hand until it dropped.

There were five letters printed deep and strong and perfect into the rafter. Printed with care. Loving care.

O LVS O

I got down and checked out the gap for the piece of mail. Gone. Down Mushrat Creek. Didn't matter. It wasn't for us anyway.

O LVS O

O for Oscar probably. Oscar loves O. Oscar loves Oscar? Oscar the mailman carved in a bridge that he loves himself?

So much that he'd climb up and sit in those rafters and carve a message to himself?

Ridiculous.

It must have been some other person named O.

I walked through our gooseberry shrubs up onto some rocks and sat under the huge butternut tree between the stand of pine and the cedar bush.

I was thinking about what I had written in the letter to Fleurette that I'd probably never send.

I wrote that if you don't take care of things they'll rust and rot away and die. Then I got an idea.

Sometimes if you write things down you get ideas you never knew you had.

Under the butternut tree I got an idea that I didn't have until that very minute.

I would be the covered bridge caretaker anyway! Maybe that way, people would notice and ...

COVERED BRIDGE HAS TWO
EXITS — BUT NO
ENTRANCE!

I was out caretaking my bridge. When I checked the lamps I worked at night.

I ran a rope from the lantern to a small pulley in the top of the portal of the bridge to another pulley between the truss and the rafters and down to a nail in one of the braces, high enough up so some little kids wouldn't untie it or fool with it and have the lamp come crashing down or set a fire or break one of their heads open.

The caretaker before me used a long wooden ladder to take care of his lamps, but it was pretty old and shaky from being out in the weather leaning on the side of the bridge for so long, so I cut it up for stove-wood and installed my pulley system in its place.

I had a lantern at each end of the bridge. The North and the South Portal.

Each end would be lit but the middle would be dark.

Unless the moon was right; then you had the patch in the middle. And, if you were lucky, maybe a ghost.

What I noticed was that the people who lived on the north side of the bridge always called the North

Portal the *entrance* and of course the other end the *exit*.

And the people on the south side of the bridge called the South Portal the *entrance* and the other end the *exit*.

To some people this could be a bit of a mix-up. For instance, one night somebody who lived on the south side of the bridge might drop in to our place and tell me that the lamp was out at the entrance of the bridge. And then a little later somebody who lived on the north side of the bridge would drop by and say that the same lamp was out at the exit of the bridge.

And if the first person stayed a bit to talk to Mrs. O'Driscoll or to O'Driscoll for a while and then the second person came along with the news about the lamp, you'd get a little argument start up because they'd both be there at once.

"It's the lamp at the exit."

"No it's not; it's the one at the entrance."

The same kind of argument that they'd maybe have over what you meant when you said *this* Sunday or if you said *next* Sunday.

"Next Sunday; is that the Sunday *coming* or is that *this* Sunday? Or is it the Sunday after next? Wait now. Is *next* Sunday the Sunday after *this* or is it *this* Sunday? Which is it?"

"The dance is next Saturday. Is that the Saturday coming or the Saturday after this?"

"It's this Saturday coming."

"Well, why didn't you say so?"

"I did. I said it was next Saturday!"

"It's *not next* Saturday then, it's this Saturday!"

On my very first Sunday working for free on the bridge, a report came that a lantern was out at one of the exits. I got my can of coal oil, my scissors and my cloth and strolled down our side road to the bridge.

It was a beautiful night, Mushrat Creek gurgling and babbling away like a baby full of milk and the Gatineau sky full of stars.

As I came up to the South Portal I could see that that light was on. It was bit sooty but it was burning.

It was the North Portal they must have said was out. I walked into the bridge and shaded my eyes from the light above me so I could see the other portal.

The moon wasn't quite right so there was no patch in the middle.

At the other end there was a light on but it wasn't in the right place. It was right close to the level of the carriageway, not up near the peak of the portal where it should have been hanging. Could it have slipped down? Broken pulley? Bad knot?

I decided to clean the South Portal light first, the one above me.

While I worked I glanced up from time to time to see the other end.

I reached up on tiptoe and untied the rope from the nail and lowered my lantern. I lifted the globe with the lever and blew out the flame. While I let the globe cool and my eyes got used to the dark, I realized the light at the other end was moving!

I pressed my back against the first timber of the truss of the bridge and let the light walk by me.

It was a man in a long robe carrying a big deer light. I knew who it was.

O'Driscoll had told me how Father Foley from our church would come over the bridge sometimes to visit the sick on Sunday nights on our side of Mushrat Creek.

I was embarrassed about hiding like that, so I said

35

very pleasantly, "Good evening, Father Foley." But because I was trying to be so natural and friendly, it came out kind of slow and spooky.

Father Foley jumped up in the air so high that on his way down his robe puffed right out like the girls' dresses did outside the Fun House at the Ottawa Exhibition when they got over that air blaster.

"Holy Mary Mother of God! Don't come up sudden on a man like that, son! Do you not know any better?"

O'Driscoll also told me how jumpy Father Foley was.

"I'm sorry, Father Foley," I said. "I was tending the light when you came along and I thought you were...I couldn't see very well...you see, the other night..."

"Well, you shouldn't be out here at all hours of the night fiddlin' around this bridge! Do you not know it's condemned — or it's goin' to be? You know you're wastin' your time, don't you? This bridge is going to be torn down! It's commendable, I suppose, you workin' without pay — I know you're not gettin' paid — but to do any caretakin' work on this bridge is fritherin' away the precious minutes God gave us on this earth that He says should be spent in fruitful labour — a sin my boy, a sin — and don't be sneakin' up on innocent people in the dark like this ... the Devil's work my boy — a sin!"

Father Foley and his light bobbed up the gravel road and round the bend and out of sight, now and then the long shadows of the plum trees darting out of the dark.

I turned up the wick in my lantern and by feeling with my fingers trimmed the burnt end square.

I shook the lantern and when I heard the slopping

sound decided that there was enough coal oil in it for now and that it was too dark to pour oil anyway.

I wiped the inside of the globe which was cool enough to touch by now and lit the lamp again and raised it to its position.

I walked slowly into the gloom of the other end, my arms and my sides tight with gooseflesh.

The other lamp hung there, dark in the rafters.

I lowered it.

It was cold. It had been out for quite a while.

I filled it by the faint light from the other end and trimmed it and wiped it and lit it and raised it.

Back home in my bedroom I looked out the window up at my bridge.

It was a dark shape that cut a horizontal line across the star-filled sky.

I went to sleep and dreamed of Sin.

COVERED BRIDGE
PLUGGED BY MANURE!

Trying to write the letter to Fleurette was getting harder and harder.

Every time I would try to tell her something, to explain something to her, I'd start to compare things to other things: I'd start to say that that thing was like this or that: or that other thing was like this.

The covered bridge is like a tunnel, I told her. But it isn't really because a tunnel goes under something and a bridge goes over. So how could you have a tunnel be like a bridge?

That's what always happened in my writing. I'd start saying one thing was like another thing but then I'd have to say that it wasn't really like that, not altogether like that, anyway, because there was always some part was maybe a little bit different.

Or the covered bridge is like a long barn with the front and the back missing and a road running through it. But there's no hay up in the loft, of course, and it's not quiet like a barn is because you can hear the water gurgling underneath and also it doesn't smell like a barn because there isn't a huge pile of cow shit out the back and I started imagining a manure pile out the South Portal with a car buried in it.

But if you're standing in the covered bridge looking out one of the vents and if it's raining and if you're watching the water passing underneath, you might feel like you're in a big tug boat on the river, but the sound of the rain on the shingles above you makes you feel like you're very cosy in a cabin somewhere in the bush beside a lake, but you have to close your eyes so you don't see the water moving under you or you'll still think it feels like a ship.

It seemed impossible to find something that was exactly like something else. Something that was exactly like a covered bridge.

In the world, there were many things that seemed to be a lot like many other things but not totally. There was always some small difference that would sort of spoil it.

Or make it not perfect.

Then I changed the subject.

I wrote to her about a habit O'Driscoll had.

O'Driscoll had a habit of turning around a bit and looking back over his shoulder just before he started to talk to you.

He didn't do it every time he said something, only when he first started to talk.

Or if he was walking up to you, meeting you on the road, just before he started to talk, he'd look behind himself, as though there might be somebody following him.

Even though he knew and the other person knew that there might not be anybody else come walking up or down that road for a half a day or more. Maybe the next person who'd come walking along that gravel road was just leaving Wakefield now and wouldn't be here until next Wednesday but O'Driscoll looked around anyway, just in case.

I don't think he knew he was doing it; it was just a habit.

He'd even do it in our kitchen when he came down for breakfast in the morning.

Mrs. O'Driscoll and I would be there and in he would come, look back over his shoulder and then start talking.

There definitely was nobody behind him because everybody who lived in the house was now in the kitchen.

Once, when O'Driscoll wasn't there, Mrs. O'Driscoll said that he probably got the habit after he was supposed to be drowned in the war and ran away and lived with that Indian Princess on Lake Pizinadjih.

She said this out of the corner of her mouth while the other half of her mouth was smiling.

I tried later to do it in the mirror; couldn't.

Didn't have the right mouth muscles, I guess.

Just then, O'Driscoll came marching into the kitchen, looked behind himself, and started talking.

"Here's how Lake Pizinadjih got its name.

"Years ago, the lake was then called Manitou, meaning Great Spirit, two Algonquin families lived across the water from each other. The son of one family fell in love with the daughter of the other family when, one evening, he heard the sound of her singing float across the sparkling moonlit surface of Manitou."

O'Driscoll was being very dramatic and Mrs. O'Driscoll was rolling her eyes which meant she'd heard this before.

O'Driscoll went ahead anyway.

"The two families hated each other for many generations and so, of course, the parents forbade the son to paddle his canoe across the water to be with his newfound love.

"The singing continued, however..."

"Of course," sighed Mrs. O'Driscoll.

"...however and after the fire died down and the family went to sleep, the son walked into the water, and began to swim, silent as a fish, to the other side and to his love.

"But it was late and the singing had stopped and the moon was now covered by cloud and the young man lost his way and swam until, exhausted, he sank and drowned."

Mrs. O'Driscoll looked at me. She had definitely heard this before.

"Days later, when they discovered his body stuck in the falls, and they figured out what happened, the two families patched up their differences and moved on together to a different place, far away, so they could forget.

"Before they left, in a carefully performed ceremony, they renamed the tragic water 'Pizinadjih.' "

Mrs. O'Driscoll — Pizinadjih. My, that's beautiful, O'Driscoll.

What does it mean, exactly, Pizinadjih?

O'Driscoll — (Pause) It means...(O'Driscoll looks behind himself). It means *"LAKE STUPID"*!

So it was the first time I talked about love in my letter to Fleurette. I decided that maybe I'd try more of it.

I told her about the ghost and O LVS O in the bridge. I told her about the priest, Father Foley, and about Sin. And about Lake Stupid.

And I told her about Old Mac Gleason, who I will tell you about now.

And about how I started going to church.

Adolf Hitler
Makes Joke!

The person after Oscar McCracken that I met in Mushrat Creek was Old Mac Gleason. He sat on his verandah across from the church and sucked on his pipe. Sometimes we would talk to him in his chair on his broken verandah. Nerves and I sometimes took a walk past there after we started going to church.

Sometimes we first went home and changed into our old clothes and we separated the milk. Of course, Nerves didn't change his clothes; he wore the same furry little suit no matter what the occasion was. But he did go to church with us sometimes. On hot summer days when there was a bit of a breeze and not too many flies, Father Foley would get the altar boys to prop the big entrance doors to the church open so the breeze would circulate while he roasted us with his sermon. But no matter how much breeze there was, once Father Foley got going about Hell, he'd be sweating like a pig.

I don't know why people say that about pigs because I don't think pigs sweat. They grunt and drool and roll around in the mud but they don't sweat much. Not nearly as much as Father Foley, especially when he got very deep into the subject of Hell.

On those hot breezy days when the doors were propped open with two rocks, Nerves would walk in very quietly and respectfully and sit in the middle of the centre aisle near the back with his paws neatly in front of him and his head up, looking at Father Foley and the boys going about their business.

During Communion, when people started getting up and filling the aisle, Nerves would back himself out the doors and go over on the lawn and take a holy little snooze there under the lilac bushes.

Old Mac Gleason could see the church and the graveyard from his chair on the verandah. Everybody knew Mac never went to church. It was pretty obvious. Everybody in Mushrat Creek, everybody in Low and everybody in Brennan's Hill who went to church got a good look every Sunday at Old Mac Gleason sitting on his verandah, *not* going to church.

And people used to say that everybody up the River in Venosta and Farrelton and Kazabazua and everybody down the River in Alcove and Wakefield probably knew that Old Mac Gleason didn't go to church.

And Old Mac Gleason himself would often say, "I betcha there's people as far south as Ottawa who know I never been to church in my life and that there's people as far north as Maniwaki that know that I, Old Mac Gleason, have no intention of ever goin' to church in the future either.

"There's people who travel miles and miles to go to a church and here's me, livin' right across the road from one — and I never been inside it. Oh, I was inside it a couple a times to fix a door or a window for that Foolish Father Foley from Farrelton but I never prayed inside there and I never will!"

43

This Sunday, Father Foley was at the top of his sermon about Hell.

The altar boys had the doors propped wide open with the rocks, and Nerves was in his position in the aisle.

Father Foley was at the part about how thick the walls of Hell were and what a foul-smelling prison it was and the lost demons and the smoke and the sulphur and the fire and the never-ending storms of brimstone and stink of the putrid corpses and vomit and boiling brains and the screaming of the tortured and cursing victims and the puddles of pus that you had to lie in if you were bad.

Father Foley had a wild look in his eyes. He looked like he was scaring himself with his own sermon.

I took a look back at Nerves.

He was staring straight up at Father Foley with a look of hopeless terror in his eyes. Was there a Hell for dogs?

It was near the end of his speech. Father Foley was sweating so much that when he threw his head to one side and then the other to say NO! NO! to the Devil, the drops of sweat flew from one side of the church to the other. The heads of the people turned this way, then that, to watch the sweat fly across.

After Mass, Nerves and I crossed the road and strolled through the graveyard. The earliest dates on the gravestones were 1848 and 1850. According to Mrs. O'Driscoll, the first Irish settlers came here in 1847. "Some of them just made it in time," she said, out of the corner of her mouth.

Other gravestones were marked 1893 and the ages were all of babies and kids. There were whole groups of them, some all from one family.

There must have been a fire or a disease.

All the names were Irish.

We went to the edge of the graveyard near the fence.

Nerves and I stopped to look for a while at one interesting gravestone with flowers on it that were pretty fresh. Maybe put there just yesterday.

The name on it was Ophelia Brown.

Ophelia Brown
Lord Have Mercy on Her, the stone said.

All around the grave were special plants and perfectly cut grass.

But there was one thing wrong.

The grave was on the other side of the page wire fence. As if the graveyard was too crowded for Ophelia Brown and they had to put it outside the fence. But the strange thing was, there was lots of room in that part of the graveyard for Ophelia Brown.

In fact Ophelia Brown was outside the section of the graveyard with hardly any graves in it at all.

I heard a cowbell ding from a field nearby and somewhere, far off, a dog barked.

Nerves was looking like he was going to burst into tears and when he gave out a little whine I decided it was time to get out of there.

We walked by Old Mac Gleason's verandah to see if he'd invite us up for a chat and a drink of water.

He did.

He gave me the pail and the dipper and I pumped some ice-cold well-water for us from his well at the side of his house.

"That Foolish Father Foley was at it again this morning, was he?" said Old Mac Gleason. "I guess he knows that Hell speech off by heart by now."

"How did you know he was talking about Hell?" I said. "Were you at church today?"

"No, I was not," said Old Mac Gleason. "Nor will I ever set foot in that place as long as I live. I don't care if it is only just across the road! But I'll tell you, there's two ways you can tell a thing like that. First of all, you watch the people coming out. The looks on their faces. Some of them look like they've just dirtied their pants and some are kind of blue around the gills and some are so guilty-looking you'd think they just took an axe to their whole family."

I waited a little bit while we listened to a heat bug singing that one note about the heat.

"What's the other way you can tell?" I said.

"The other way you can tell," he said, leaning right over to Nerves and me, "is that you can hear the old fool from all the way over here!"

Then he looked up and over at the graveyard so steadily that Nerves and I looked over too.

There was a man at Ophelia Brown's grave, kneeling there, with flowers in his hands. He crossed himself and then he got up and replaced the flowers that were there with the new ones.

Then he knelt again and kissed the ground.

"Know who that is?" asked Old Mac Gleason.

It was too far away to make out the man's face but the way his back was humped over looked sort of familiar.

"You know the postman, don't you? Oscar McCracken? He's just finished the Sunday mail. He's also our grave-digger, did you know that?"

I could tell now it was Oscar McCracken the way he was walking now away from Ophelia Brown's grave with his head down, watching his shoes.

"Strange rig, that one. A queer duck, that's for

sure," said Old Mac Gleason. "When you get to know Mushrat Creek a little better you'll find out more than you'll ever need to know about strange rigs like that Oscar McCracken and his grave outside the fence...you know you're the first strangers that have come in to live here for a good while now. You think you'll settle here? You could find a better spot than beside that old broken-down covered bridge...say, that's a funny lookin' dog—what kind of a dog is that anyway—or is it a dog at all—sure, it looks more like a—I don't know what the hell it looks like come to think of it ..."

Just then, Mrs. O'Driscoll came along, calling to us from the road. She had been up a ways, visiting after church.

Mrs. O'Driscoll and I and Nerves walked across the covered bridge to our mailbox.

Was there a letter there from Fleurette Featherstone Fitchell? There wasn't, but there was a seed catalogue for Mrs. O'Driscoll and a Police Gazette for O'Driscoll.

At least some of our family was getting some mail.

O'Driscoll looked forward to getting his Police Gazette every two weeks or so. He would save it for Sunday and take it into the parlour after church and sit down in there and read it.

Nobody went in there very often unless maybe there was a visitor in the house. But O'Driscoll liked to go in there on Sunday when his shoes were shined and he had on his white shirt and tie. Sometimes I went in with my *War and Peace* and sat there with him and read silently there, sitting on the chair with the big sunflowers that matched the couch that O'Driscoll was on.

The parlour smelled of sweet dust and old bread dough. It was very quiet in there. Except for the ticking of the clock on the fake mantelpiece. There were two big old photographs in round frames on the walls, a yellowish colour, a man and a woman, stiff collars, sour faces. And one square photograph of a little kid who looked like he hated his clothes. There was something wrong with his face, though. I couldn't figure out what it was. Then O'Driscoll told me one time while we were having breakfast.

He told me that in the old days it took a long time to take a picture.

You had to stay perfectly still for quite a while to get your picture taken because of the way the first cameras were made.

You couldn't smile for that long because your face would get too sore.

That's why everybody in those old pictures looks so grumpy.

Even the little kids.

One Sunday, O'Driscoll was reading his Police Gazette and I was reading my *War and Peace*. I was reading the part where Prince Andrei was retreating from Napoleon in the War of 1812. He was leading his regiment through the dust in August in Russia. And they came along to a lake and all his men stripped off their clothes and jumped in the water. Then somebody yelled out that Prince Andrei might want to have a swim. So they all got out of the water to let their prince get in and take a swim. And Prince Andrei went in but he was embarrassed about taking off his clothes in front of his men.

It was in Book II, Part II, Chapter 5.

On the front page of O'Driscoll's Police Gazette there was a picture of Adolf Hitler, the German who started the war in 1939 that O'Driscoll got lost in. After the war was over they looked all over for Hitler but they couldn't find him. Most people said he committed suicide and his friends burned his body.

Nice to have friends. Even if you're Hitler.

But O'Driscoll's Police Gazette was saying that Hitler was still alive. On the front page there was a big picture of Hitler with his little moustache and a big headline saying the words, "Hitler Is Alive!" The story in the smaller print said that a barber in a country called Patagonia in South America said that Hitler came into his barber shop and got his moustache shaved off. The barber said that Hitler seemed to be bit fatter than he was when he was losing the war that he started, but that he seemed quite cheerful and even made a few jokes.

"You can't win 'em all!" the barber said Hitler said.

O'Driscoll left the parlour to go out to the outhouse, and while he was gone I found out one of his secrets.

I was looking through his Police Gazette, taking a break from *War and Peace*, reading the stories in there. A story about a two-headed parrot. One head would tell a joke and the other head would laugh. Or one head would say, "Why did the parrot cross the road?" And the other head would say, "I dunno. Why did the parrot cross the road?" And the first head would say, "To get to the other side!" And then both heads would laugh their heads off.

And there was a story about a guy in Madagascar or somewhere who found an oyster with not a pearl in it but a whole pearl necklace. But when he took it to the jeweller's, they said the pearls were just imitation pearls, just fake.

Then on the next page there was a story about a drowning sailor being saved by a dolphin.

The sailor fell overboard and swam around for a long time and just as he was going to sink and drown because he was so tired a dolphin swam under him and with the sailor on its back, swam to a beautiful tropical island with the sailor. And the sailor got off there and got married to the Queen of the Amazons and became King of Paradise.

The thing about this story was that O'Driscoll told me and Mrs. O'Driscoll just the other day that that's what happened to him when he was supposed to be drowned in the War. That was the latest he told us. Then he said he *thought* that that was what must have happened because he lost his memory don't forget so he couldn't really be sure.

So O'Driscoll was stealing his stories from the Police Gazette. Telling me and Mrs. O'Driscoll stuff about when he was lost in the war. Getting the ideas from his Police Gazette.

No wonder he only half listened to my tale about a ghost.

But I had other things on my mind.

Things like initials.

O LVS O, for instance.

It had to be Oscar Loves Ophelia.

It had to be.

Man Digs a Hole
Then Can't Get Out!

I never went to church much when I lived in Lowertown or when I lived in Uplands Emergency Shelter but now that I was living on Mushrat Creek I was going to church almost every Sunday.

It was good to go and hear what everybody was saying about everything. And it felt good to get dressed up on Sunday morning after you did the milking and the separating and you fed the pigs and checked the henhouse for eggs.

At first O'Driscoll tried to get Mrs. O'Driscoll to polish our Sunday shoes and put them on the kitchen table so that when we slept in on Sunday morning we could come downstairs and jump right into these clean shiny shoes and head right out for church with no "delays."

O'Driscoll told her that all the other farmers' wives in Mushrat Creek did that for *their* husbands and their sons. He told her that it was a tradition. Then he told her more of what the other women did for their men on Sundays. They got up at five o'clock in the morning, made the fire, got the breakfast, heated up the iron, sponged and ironed the men's pants, ironed clean white shirts for the men, got out the tie they always wore on Sunday, went out and milked the cows, separated the milk, fed the pigs, checked for eggs in the henhouse, came back in, got out the good shoes, cleaned and polished them and then put them in a neat, side-by-side way, right beside the breakfast on the table.

While O'Driscoll was explaining this to Mrs. O'Driscoll, she just stared at him. She didn't really stare at him, she just calmly looked at him for the whole time he was telling her all this stuff about what she was supposed to do on Sunday morning for her *men*!

It was pretty cruel, really.

She didn't say a word, just looking at him, like maybe the way you'd look at a sunset or something.

And the whole time, you could tell, O'Driscoll was wishing she would say something, because if she started talking, then he could stop talking, but as long as she didn't talk at all, he had to keep talking. And the more he talked the worse everything got. It was like watching a cat play with a mouse.

Mrs. O'Driscoll used to call it "the silence." If O'Driscoll was getting a bit too "cocky," she would give him "the silence."

And it seemed to work every time.

O'Driscoll would get more and more excited and say things that got worse and worse.

Mrs. O'Driscoll said once that it was like watching a man dig himself into a deep hole. "You let them dig until they can't get out. Then you wait a while and then you help them get out," she said.

O'Driscoll was telling her about how it was a mortal sin not to shine your husband's Sunday shoes and that a lot of women up and down the Gatineau Valley were in Hell because they didn't shine their husband's Sunday shoes or if they weren't in Hell already, "they were definitely headed in that direction..."

Mrs. O'Driscoll waited a while and then she gave him a little tiny smile that you could hardly notice. This was the way she helped him out of the hole he was in.

Then she handed him the shoe polish.

He took the polish and gave me a big wink.

The wink was the way he helped himself the rest of the way out of the hole.

After church at home, Mrs. O'Driscoll was putting on her overalls which she never did on Sunday.

"Put on your workin' clothes, Hubbo me boy," she said. "We're goin' to do a little paintin'."

"Painting?" I said. "Painting what?"

"Your bridge, my boy," she said out of the corner of her mouth. "Your bridge."

"We can't paint that bridge. It's too big. You'd need dozens of cans of paint and scaffolds and rope and all kinds of things."

"We're only going to paint what we can reach, boy. I've been out gossiping. I heard the priest's housekeeper telling them all what Father Foley said to you that night about workin' on the bridge and Sin and all that. That's wrong, Hubbo. Very wrong. You're not sinning to work for your beliefs. So just to show who's side I'm on, let them have a look at us paintin' this bridge, the both of us. Maybe by the example we set, others will join us and the bridge will be looked at as something worth saving!"

We got some painting done, but not much. Mrs. O'Driscoll only had a small can of red paint and one good brush, so we took turns.

"It's the thought that counts," Mrs. O'Driscoll was saying, as she hummed a little while I took my turn painting the tongue-in-groove sheeting on the outside of the trellis. I was leaning over the railing while standing on the abutment at our end of the bridge.

"I said I was out gossiping, Hubbo. But I've been doin' more than that. I've been listening."

"Listening?"

"Yes, my dear Hubbo. A tragic thing happened in this community over fifteen years ago. It involved the daughter of a poor woman I met up the road last Sunday, Mrs. Brown. Her daughter died. Her daughter, Ophelia, who was very young and full of hope, died."

"Ophelia Brown," I said. "I saw her gravestone. And Oscar McCracken..."

"Yes, Oscar the mailman was her betrothed."

"How did she die?" I asked.

"Brain tumour," she said.

Oscar McCracken and Ophelia Brown were lovers. This was almost twenty years ago. They were going to be married. Suddenly everything changed. Ophelia Brown started acting strange. She went kind of crazy. Looking around as though people were following her. Not talking to her friends. In the church three or four times a day. The tumour affected her brain. They found her in Mushrat Creek. She must have jumped out the ventilation window in the middle of the covered bridge. It was in the early spring. The water was roaring high almost over the centre pier. She must have hit her head. Anyway, she was drowned. Father Foley wouldn't give her a proper funeral. He was a young priest then. He had to follow the rules. His hands were tied. Wouldn't let her be buried in the churchyard. Against God's rules, he said. Oscar McCracken started going around watching his feet. Got a hump

54

on his back from it. Ophelia wasn't allowed in the graveyard. She was buried just outside the fence.

We took a break from painting and I showed Mrs. O'Driscoll the initials up in the rafters.

We went in and put the rest of our little bit of paint on the outside boards around the vent where Ophelia Brown had jumped.

The paint lasted a tiny bit longer than it would have because Mrs. O'Driscoll watered it down with some of her tears.

"F"–Word Linked
to Priest!

My letter to Fleurette was getting fatter.

I was telling her about everything.

I was trying to tell Fleurette all about Father Foley and how Old Mac Gleason called him Foolish Father Foley and that Father Foley was from the town of Farrelton just north of Low up the road and how Old Mac Gleason called him Foolish Father Foley from Farrelton, which sounded funny because of all the F's.

And I wondered while I was writing to her about him what Foolish Father Foley from Farrelton would say to Fleurette Featherstone Fitchell about Hell and what she should do and what she shouldn't do.

Lucky that Father Foley couldn't read people's minds, because if he could and he read my mind in church when I was thinking about Fleurette, he'd probably blast me right straight to Hell for having such thoughts.

Funny part of it was that it was Father Foley who got me started thinking about Sin in the first place. If you yell and scream about Sin all the time, people are going to start thinking about things that they never thought of before.

Fortunately for Fleurette Featherstone Fitchell, Foolish Father Foley from Farrelton was far from fixing her with his fault-finding.

I put that sentence with all the F words in the letter.

Fleurette would like that one.

If I ever found her address.

I also told her as much as I could about Oscar McCracken.

Everybody loved Oscar McCracken.

One of the reasons was that he never missed the mail. He was always on time. He was as regular as the train. When you heard him pull up in his coupe car and when you heard your mailbox squeak (or whatever it did — some mailboxes squealed like little pigs, some groaned like cows, some went chunk like an axe hitting wood), then you knew just about what exact time it was, and you thought of what a nice man Oscar was.

Everybody also loved Oscar because most of the time, maybe all the time, the mail he brought them was nice mail — a letter from a relative from the States; a parcel from Sears or Eaton's, a notice saying pick up that sack of seeds you ordered. (Was I the only one that never got what he wanted from Oscar? A letter from Fleurette?)

And also, everybody loved Oscar because everybody knew what happened to Ophelia Brown and everybody knew how it changed Oscar forever. Everybody knew how he felt. How he got the hump on his back from watching his feet.

And everybody knew that whenever Oscar went through the covered bridge he would stay inside there for a while and have a little chat with Ophelia Brown.

But not very many people talked about what Oscar used to do four times a day inside the bridge. Everybody knew that he'd stop for a bit and have a little chat with his lost lover Ophelia, but because it seemed a little bit crazy they didn't like to mention it much. They didn't like to come right out and say that Oscar McCracken talked to a ghost four times a day.

And I didn't like to say that maybe I saw that ghost one night.

O LVS O. That's what the bridge said.

If they said that, then they'd have to say they believed there was a ghost there or say that Oscar was crazy. They couldn't say right out that they believed Ophelia's ghost was there in the covered bridge because if Foolish Father Foley got wind of the fact that they believed in ghosts, especially in Ophelia Brown's ghost, he would get pretty mad and go into a rage about Evil and everything. Father Foley already kept her out of the graveyard and anyway, Father Foley was in charge of things like ghosts and spirits and he'd be the one to decide about stuff like that. It wasn't the farmers who were going to decide about things like that. Farmers were in charge of cows and milk and manure and seeds and hay and homemade bread and chickens and things like that.

Foolish Father Foley from Farrelton was in charge of the other world.

That is why when people heard the covered bridge was going to be torn down everybody got very confused.

First of all nobody wanted to talk about Oscar McCracken and Ophelia Brown. If the bridge was torn down, what would happen to poor Oscar? Poor Oscar who everybody loved?

It was O'Driscoll who was one of the first ones to get into the mix-up.

"What was wrong with having two bridges?" O'Driscoll was saying to farmers in the store in Brennan's Hill. "One for the past, one for the future?"

Then I wrote about Oscar's goat to Fleurette.

After Mass one day when Mrs. Ball invited Mrs. O'Driscoll to walk back down the road with her and drop into her niece's place and have some tea, Mr. O'Driscoll and I and Nerves crossed the road for a stroll through the graveyard and then past Old Mac Gleason's house. I noticed from the graveyard that the sexton's cottage where Oscar kept the church equipment and graveyard tools had a pen and a small stable behind it that you couldn't see from the church. In the pen was a goat.

O'Driscoll started the conversation with Old Mac Gleason about the goat.

"You know goats are thought to have originated in China some ten million years ago." O'Driscoll sounded like he just read a sentence from a school book about goats.

"Well, sir," said Old Mac Gleason, "this goat originated here as a kid and belonged to poor Ophelia Brown. After she died, Oscar took the goat and still has it. As a matter of fact, Father Foley hired Oscar as the sexton so the goat would keep the grass cut. Shows you how much that Foolish Father Foley knows about goats! Goats aren't lawnmowers! Wasn't long until he had the pen built, though. One day the goat marched right down the aisle into the middle of Father Foley's sermon and started bleating away like she was saying what everybody else felt like saying—"Shut up, you old blatherskite Father

Foley"—bleating away at him. The look on Father Foley's face! And the terror in the eyes! You'd think he was staring at the Devil himself!

"There's nothing Father Francis Foley from Farrelton hates worse than having his speeches about Sin interrupted. But that Oscar, he knows goats. Watch the way he feeds that thing. Nothing but the best. Goes out every now and then with that little car and loads it up with the kind of grub the goat loves. Pine branches, young bark, wild roses, clover. And milks her every twelve hours. I never seen a goat live so long. And keep givin' milk, too! Nice fresh goat's milk keeps that Father Foley nice and fat! I wonder, Mr. O'Driscoll, you being a man who has travelled widely and knowing a lot about a lot of things, do you think that too much goat's milk could affect a fat priest's brain? Make him crazy?"

"No, Mr. Gleason," said Mr. O'Driscoll. "I don't know anything about that, but I *do* know that the animal called the goat was always hooked up with Sin in the olden days. The old Hebrews in ancient times used to bring two goats to the altar. Then they'd draw lots. One goat went to the Lord and the other to the Devil. That one they called the scapegoat. Then the priest would confess all his sins and the sins of all the people. Then because all the sins were now with the scape-goat, they'd take it out in the bush and let it get away, let it escape."

Like everybody always was when O'Driscoll told one of his stories, Old Mac Gleason was silent and a bit amazed.

We listened for a while to the polite Sunday morning birds.

"Well, anyways," Old Mac Gleason said, "that Oscar, he is a queer duck himself since his lady did herself in. Rings the church bell, does the chores, takes the collection, delivers the mail, digs the graves. Never talks to anybody. Strangest package of a man I ever saw!"

I was starting not to like Old Mac Gleason.

O'Driscoll and Nerves and I crossed back over the road and cut in behind the church in back of the sexton's cottage where the goat pen was.

The goat was black with a white face and white legs and a white beard. She had two black tassles hanging from her throat and curved black horns. Her udder was swollen and her teats pointed straight and were stiff. She was full of milk.

She had a funny look on her face. She looked like a person looks who just pasted a "kick-me" sign on your back and is trying not to laugh while looking you right in the eye.

Suddenly she turned her eyes on Nerves and bleated once at him. Her eyes turned piercing and cold.

Nerves went roaring down the road in a little chuckwagon of dust.

O'Driscoll and I laughed all the way home. We laughed at the goat bleating at Father Foley and at the goat bleating at Nerves. And we laughed at Old Mac Gleason.

Fleurette would like this part of the letter.

DOG ATTACKED BY
KILLER POTATO BUGS!

Father Foley was doing something to my mind. For instance, even something that happened to Nerves made me think of Father Foley's sermons.

It was Nerves who first noticed that our potato field was being attacked by bugs. The potato plants were quite high when we took over the farm. Our field was outside our front door and across our side road. We had twelve rows of potatoes, twenty paces long. Since there are about four potato plants in every long pace, there must have been almost a thousand potato plants. More potatoes than we'd ever need. But we could use them for trading for other things we didn't have.

I saw Nerves come out of the potato field through the barbed wire gate. He was looking pretty disgusted. His skin was moving up and down his body. He was shuddering like someone in a restaurant who just found a cockroach crawling out of his spaghetti.

I went into the potato field to see what it was that made Nerves so nauseated.

On the first potato plant I inspected I counted

fifty-six fat orange potato bugs with black spots, munching away on the leaves.

The next plant had even more.

Now I realized what was bothering Nerves.

Nerves hated bugs of all kinds. He always avoided flies, spiders, moths, butterflies, grasshoppers, ants, any kind of bug, whenever he could.

I guess he was just out for a stroll in the potato patch when he looked around and realized that he was surrounded by over 55,000 bugs. And all related to each other. Poor Nerves was outnumbered.

I got some empty Habitant Pea Soup cans that were piled on a shelf in our shed just next to the potato field.

By holding a Habitant Pea Soup can under the leaf of the potato plant and using a flat stick, you could knock the bugs into the can.

At first they made a pinging noise when they hit the bottom of the can, but then things got quieter and more disgusting as the can filled up.

I put the first full can on the gatepost and started a new one. I was starting to feel like Nerves must have felt, his skin crawling up and down his body.

Mrs. O'Driscoll came up to the gate with Nerves behind her.

She pulled on the gate but it stuck a bit, so she yanked a little harder. That caused the Habitant Pea Soup can, full to the top with potato bugs, to fall off the gatepost, dumping most of the bugs on top of Nerves.

Nerves was stunned. He stood still as a statue while the bugs spread over his body like bees. Nerves' eyes, which normally were kind of beady, were wider than Mrs. O'Driscoll or I had ever seen them. It didn't seem possible that his eyes could expand and bulge out like that.

Then his mouth opened wide like he was screaming, but no sound was coming out.

Then he took off as fast as his little legs could churn and kick up grass and dirt, down around the ice house, and we heard the splash as Nerves hit the water of Mushrat Creek.

"Well," said Mrs. O'Driscoll out of the corner of her mouth, "we'll find out now if potato bugs can swim or not."

We ended up with seven cans of potato bugs.

The stove in the summer kitchen was roaring hot, ready for baking bread.

Mrs. O'Driscoll and I dumped the bugs into the flames. What a stink for a while.

I couldn't help thinking about Father Foley.

The stink and the flames.

Of Hell.

WOMAN BUILDS BRIDGE!

Not long after we heard the first dynamite go off and saw the first dead fish float down Mushrat Creek, a poster went up in the store at Brennan's Hill.

MEN WANTED
BRIDGE CONSTRUCTION
MUSHRAT CREEK

Carpentry, Cement, Steel,
Laborers.
THE LAZY NEED NOT APPLY!

Madame Ovide Proulx
Proulx Construction

A lot of farmers were crowded around the poster. They read "Madame Ovide Proulx." *Madame* Proulx? A *woman*?

A *woman* building a bridge?

How could that *be*?

O'Driscoll and I went up to the place where the new bridge was going to be.

It was an ugly sight.

Blown-up trees and bulldozers and mud and big gashes out of the sides of beautiful Mushrat Creek.

O'Driscoll got in a line-up and got hired on as a carpenter. While he was signing his work card I saw him saying something to the woman in charge. She looked up at me. Then O'Driscoll waved for me to come over.

"Madame Proulx wants to hire you. She needs a nail puller. You get eighty cents an hour. You work from seven in the morning until six at night, one hour for lunch, only half days on Saturday."

Mrs. Proulx looked at me.

"Can you pull nails?" she said.

"Out of wood?" I said.

"Of course, out of wood. What did you tink, you pull dem hout of da hair?"

"Pardon?"

"Did you think you'll pull them out of the air?" O'Driscoll said, helping me out.

"Yes, I can pull nails," I said, ignoring her sarcasm.

"Sign ere!" said Mrs. Proulx.

I had a job.

I was already figuring out the money. Ten hours a day would be eight dollars. Five times eight. Four more dollars for Saturday. Forty-four dollars a week! I could buy more red paint with that. And other stuff for the bridge — lamp oil, wicks.

We started work the next day.

For the next few days, before I went to bed, I'd try to tell Fleurette about what it was like.

A farmer or two from almost every house along the road and by the river and up and down the valley were working on the new bridge.

There was rock and earth to be moved and holes to be dug and forms to be built and cement to be poured and steel to be laid.

The foreman of the job was French and he was from Maniwaki. His name was printed on the side of the truck and the end of the big generator. His name was Ovide Proulx (pronounced PROO).

His wife, Mrs. Proulx (pronounced PROO, too) was in charge of the Time, the Tools and Supplies and the Pay Envelopes.

All the farmers called her Prootoo.

On Fridays, Prootoo rang the bell at six o'clock sharp and the farmers lined up in their blue overalls and waited while she called out their names and made them step up for their envelope of money. She also sometimes searched the farmers for stolen tools or nails.

Sometimes there was money taken out of the farmers' pay envelopes for a tool they maybe lost or broke.

Everybody was afraid of Prootoo.

Except Mr. Proulx, the boss.

And everybody hated Prootoo.

Except Mr. Ovide Proulx. He loved Prootoo.

Whenever he went away in the truck he kissed her on the cheek and when he got back a little later, he kissed her again. And even while he was kissing her on the cheek, she turned her head so that she never took her eyes off the farmers as they slowly built the new bridge.

She never took her eyes off the farmers as they slowly built the bridge from seven o'clock in the morning to six o'clock at night except on Saturday, and then it was eight o'clock in the morning to twelve o'clock noon that she *never never* stopped watching.

Just before the twelve o'clock dinner bell one of the farmers who was swinging a sledge hammer let it go and it flew out and landed in the deep part of Mushrat Creek.

Prootoo was already marching over to where the farmer and I were standing even before the hammer hit the water.

"You go in and get it," said Prootoo, pointing at the farmer who let go the hammer. "Take off your overalls, jump in the creek, get the sledge 'ammer."

I could see the hammer down there, through the clear water, the hammer head on the bottom in the mud, the handle pointing straight up, floating.

I could see by the farmer's face, he wasn't going to take off his overalls for her or anybody else.

"You want to work?" she said to him. "Let's get in dat water!"

I knew the farmer was going to get fired.

I took a chance.

"I'll go," I said.

"O.K.," she said. "Fine. Let's go before it sinks in the mud!"

I was fiddling with the strap of my overalls, waiting to see if she would stop staring and look away. I got the strap undone and looked up again. Prootoo was still staring. She had the dinner bell in her hand. It was almost past twelve o'clock and all the hungry farmers were standing around staring at her, waiting for her to ring the bell.

My fingers went up to my other strap and I looked up again, wondering if she was going to turn her back while I took off my pants.

All the farmers stood around where the new bridge was going to be, all the farmers, still as statues, waiting for my pants to go down, waiting for the bell, waiting for their dinner, their stomachs groaning and rumbling.

I was thinking of Prince Andrei, how he felt.

If Prince Andrei could do it, so could I...

I couldn't write any more in Fleurette's letter. I

was falling out of the chair I was so tired. I could finish it later. Working ten hours in a row every day makes you tired.

I lay down on the straw mattress that Mrs. O'Driscoll had fixed up and sank softly into it. I only had to move a couple of spikes of stubble sticking in me before I was comfortable. The mattress cover smelled clean like the breeze off Mushrat Creek. And because of the fresh straw, my whole bed had a smell of sweet dust and clover.

HORSEBALLS ROLL
DOWN MAN'S CHEEKS!

On the first Sunday of my first week working on the new bridge, I went exploring.

Past the woodpile on the south side of our house, along the road between the barn and the stable, past the manure pile and the pig pen, past the strawberry patch and through the pine bush, down along our lower field and the ancient rail fence and onto the log road that led to the river, Nerves and I walked east.

It was called the log road because the lower swampy parts were made of logs, lying crossways, lodged in the clay and mud.

As the road moved up rocky hills and down into meadows and gullies and through pine and spruce bush, you could sometimes hear Mushrat Creek talking away as it wandered near us.

Further on, the tall thick sumac with the sickening blood-red fruit blocked off all sound except for the summer heat bugs.

And later, we edged sideways down the clay, and then passed through the dark bark and the white berries of the poison dogwood trees.

Then over the last rocky part to the water, feeling

70

your feet squishing on the stinkhorn fungus until you and your totally disgusted dog reached the hemlock tree where the rowboat was pulled up and tied with a chain.

And then if you looked north up the Gatineau River, past where Mushrat Creek dumped in its pretty water, you would be able to see (but you couldn't, because the river turned there) Devil's Hole and the dam at Low.

I pulled the boat up a bit more, bailed it out with an old dented dipper that I found under the back seat.

I was thinking that if O'Driscoll and Mrs. O'Driscoll bought this farm, then this shoreline, these rocks, this boat, this hemlock tree that was supposed to be poisonous would all be ours.

I wondered if the water was ours too. Probably not.

Out in the middle of the river there were two people in a big rowboat.

You could hear them talking, and by the sounds they were making you could tell they were working at something, something heavy.

They were lifting something big and brown.

There was a man who had most of the weight and a boy, maybe his son, helping him.

What they were resting on the side of the boat now was a wood stove. It was about the size of our wood stove — four lids, an oven and a reservoir plus legs. The stove was very rusty and was breaking up a bit as they rested it on the gunwale of the boat.

Then Nerves and I heard the man count one, two, three, GO!

And over into the Gatineau River went the rusty stove.

A puff of red dust, probably rust, rose up, and the

stove sank almost right away. A dirty little geyser of water shot up as the river swallowed.

Then there was some shouting and some crying.

Then the man and the boy both peered silently over the edge of the boat into the water.

Then they started tossing in the long, sausage, hollow pieces. The stove pipes. They were easy. And the lids.

I was imagining exactly what they could see. The stove lids taking longer to disappear because of the seesaw motion they made while they were sinking, like plates.

The rusty trail of large then smaller air pockets.

And I was imagining what they couldn't see.

The stove hitting bottom softly, bouncing over on its side, settling in.

To stay there for years.

But just *before* they dumped the stove, something happened.

There was some grunting caused by lifting.

Then the man was saying something like "lift your end, lift, lift!"

Then the stove went over.

But the boy must have hurt himself or cut himself or something because his both hands were down now holding his ankle and his head was a way back, his face facing the sky.

"Stop that! What happened? Let me see," the man was saying. "What are you crying for? What's this crying? Stop it! Be a man! Stop being a baby! Be a man! Don't cry! Be a man!"

I was remembering that only last year I cried. I cried about something I did that I was ashamed of and also because an old lady who was a friend of mine died. I cried and Mrs. O'Driscoll didn't say, "be a man!" She didn't say that. She put her arms around me and gave me a big long hug. I was wondering about Mrs. O'Driscoll when she was a little girl. Did she once cry and did somebody come along and say, "Stop that! Be a woman! Don't cry! Be a woman!"?

It seemed stupid to me. Why should the boy be a man? And what if he was a man? Men cry. I saw O'Driscoll cry. He cried the night he came home from being lost in the War. While he was crying, Mrs. O'Driscoll didn't run over to him and yell at him and tell him he shouldn't be crying because he was a man!

He cried and while we were watching him he started to laugh at the same time he was crying.

I heard him the other day telling one of the farmers at the bridge about it. "There I was," he said, "crying away, tears as big as horseballs rolling down my cheeks!"

In the parlour that afternoon, while we were reading, O'Driscoll looked up suddenly and said this: "I've got, I think, a good plan to save your bridge. You and Mrs. O'Driscoll have won over some of the people with your paintin' and your fixin'. Some of the farmers at the Brennan's Hill Hotel are sympathetic to the cause. But not all of them are, Hubbo. And when it comes down to the money, the few you've won over will give in. No sir, we need a stronger position. If it touches their pockets they'll buckle under."

"What are you going to do?" I said.

"Start a petition. Get a petition signed by every workin' man on the job is what I'm going to do, me lad! Get a list of names of everybody on the job saying they want the old bridge saved to show their children and their children's children how they used to live!"

Baby Tells Lies
Before It Can Talk!

Prootoo and I were getting along fairly well. At least when she looked at me, her eyes seemed kinder than before. And the day that Mrs. O'Driscoll brought her the homemade black currant jam, she almost smiled at me.

There were farmers of all sizes working on the bridge. Small farmers, medium-sized farmers, big farmers.

The biggest farmer of them all looked like he was wearing shoulder pads under his shirt. He reminded me of a football player who played for the Ottawa Rough Riders named Tony Golab. We used to wait outside the little door in the green fence at half time for the players to come back on the field. There was a cement ledge you could stand on, and when Tony Golab came by I once jumped on his back and rode him into the park without paying.

"Hang on, kid!" he said while the security guard was trying to pull me off him. "Hang on, kid!" he said.

His sweater was covered with mud so you couldn't see his number. But I knew what it was. It was 72.

And there was blood on his cheek.

The biggest farmer of them all reminded me of Tony Golab.

Another one of the farmers liked to sing.

He had only one song but it had hundreds of verses. They were all about some ancient guy named Brian O'Lynn.

The verses sounded like this:

Oh, Brian O'Lynn and his wife and wife's mother
Tried to go over the bridge together
The storm it was howling, the bridge it fell in.
"We'll go home by water," says Brian O'Lynn.

But our most famous farmer was not working on the bridge at all.

He was a visitor who came over during our lunch hour and entertained us while we lay on the ground, sprawled out on the ground, full of food and resting.

Everybody said that Old Mickey Malarkey was the biggest liar on the Gatineau River. The Gatineau River runs from north of the town of Maniwaki right down to Ottawa. There are lots of little towns and villages in the Gatineau River Valley and lots of farms and houses along the river.

There were lots of liars living between Maniwaki and Ottawa. Maybe hundreds of liars. And so to be the biggest liar in the whole valley you had to be very good at it. There was quite a lot of competition.

Old Mickey Malarkey was the best.

He was also the one who had the most practice because he was the oldest. Old Mickey Malarkey was 112 years old and the farmers all said that he'd been lying since he was a little baby. Some of the farmers working on the new bridge said that Old Mickey Malarkey was lying before he learned to talk, if you can imagine that.

Old Mickey Malarkey was lying away back in the 1840's. Before Canada was even a country — before Confederation. Before the invention of the radio, the telephone, the car, before electricity. Old Mickey Malarkey was telling lies when my favourite writer, Leo Tolstoy, who wrote *War and Peace*, was only about twelve years old.

Whenever anybody asked Old Mickey Malarkey about being the biggest liar in the Gatineaus, he would say that he never told a lie in his life, which, of course, was one of the biggest big lies he ever told.

You could see the top of Old Mickey's house from where we were building the new bridge.

About a quarter to twelve Old Mickey would leave his house, and by the time Prootoo rang the bell at twelve noon, he was already shuffling along the road. By the time most of the farmers were finished eating, Mickey would finally arrive.

Most everybody would be sprawled out on their backs with their arms and legs spread out and their mouths open and their eyes half shut. And their stomachs swelling up and down, trying to digest all the food they ate and all the tea and water they drank.

It would take Old Mickey about forty-five minutes to walk that far. I could probably walk from his house to where we had our dinner in about thirty seconds.

I told O'Driscoll one day that I could probably throw a stone that far.

"But, Hubbo, you're young. You know, he's pretty near a hundred years older than you. They tell me around here that fifty years ago, when your covered bridge was built, Old Mickey was sixty-two years of age. In fact, he was the foreman on the job.

He's built many barns in his day, and so building a covered bridge is almost the same. Now, Hubbo, when you're — what is it he is, let's see — when *you're* one hundred and twelve years of age, I hope you can do as well!"

When Old Mickey finally got there he sat on a saw-horse or a bag of cement and got his breath and then he got up and walked around through the bodies of the farmers. He was bent over quite a bit and his hands were holding each other behind his back.

Then he started. It was a game they all knew. A conversation game.

"Went out last night after dark on the river. Stayed about an hour. *Filled* the boat with catfish!" said Old Mickey Malarkey.

"*Filled* the boat, Mickey?" said one farmer who was lying on his back with his arms out and his legs apart.

"Well, filled a *tub* and a couple of buckets."

"A *tub* and a couple of buckets, Mickey?" said another farmer, lying on his stomach with his face on his arm.

"O.K., a *tub* then. A *tub full*," said Mickey.

"A *tub full*, Mickey?" another farmer said, steam rising from him.

"Well, it was *half* full," said Mickey.

"*Half* full, Mickey?" another farmer said, pouring water over his head to cool off.

"Well, it was dark. But there were a *lot* of fish in there."

"A *lot* of fish, Mickey?" said the biggest farmer of them all.

"O.K. *Some* fish. *Some*."

"*Some* fish, Mickey?" said O'Driscoll.

"Well, say, half *a dozen* or so."

"*Or so*, Mickey?" said the first farmer.

"O.K. Two. Two nice big catfish."

"Two, Mickey?" said farmer number two.

"All right. One. One *huge* catfish. The biggest catfish I ever saw. Huge."

"Huge, Mickey?" said the wet farmer.

"A good size, a fair-sized fish."

"Fair size, Mickey?" said O'Driscoll.

"O.K. It was a small one. They weren't biting, it's the moon or something. I threw it back."

"Did you catch *any* fish Mickey?" I felt like saying, but the singing farmer beat me to it.

"No! I didn't catch one damn fish. Are you satisfied?"

"Did you even *go* fishing, Mickey?" somebody finally said.

"No! I didn't go fishing. I hate fishing. And I hate catfish. They're ugly and they scare me. As a matter of fact I've heard tell that they're poison. The Devil put them there in the river!"

"You're an awful liar, Mickey Malarkey. An awful liar!"

Just then Prootoo came along and announced that we were going to tear down the covered bridge as soon as one lane of the new bridge was laid.

It was in the contract.

It couldn't be helped.

The way she said that it couldn't be helped, you could tell she was sort of sorry.

But business was business.

BOY APPOINTED
KING OF MUSHRAT CREEK!

I was learning a lot on my new job.

One of the first things I learned was that I wasn't going to earn forty-four dollars a week because I wasn't going to be able to work every day.

When I ran out of nails to pull, Prootoo would come up and say, "You're laid off. Come back tomorrow. We might 'ave some more cloux for you!" She would laugh when she said that. Then, I noticed that she was calling me "Cloux," which is the French word for nail. But it wasn't in a mean way.

"Hey, Cloux! You're laid off! Come back tomorrow. See if dere's any cloux for you!" I was the only one on the job she joked with.

Mrs. O'Driscoll said she didn't have any kids of her own and she liked me because I was adopted.

"How did she know I was adopted?" I asked Mrs. O'Driscoll.

"Why I told her, of course," said Mrs. O'Driscoll out of the corner of her mouth.

Another thing I learned was about whistling. One of the smaller farmers was helping with the pulling of the nails one day. Actually, he was banging the dried cement off the wood so I could get at the nails. He was whistling a song. He was whistling "I been workin' on the railroad." Just to be friendly, I started whistling the same song. Whistling "I been workin' on the railroad" right along with him. He stopped whistling and stopped banging the cement off his board and stared at me.

"You don't whistle the same song at the same time another person is whistling the song. Don't you know that?"

I apologized. I didn't know that.

You can learn a lot while you're building a bridge.

On one of my laid-off days (I called them cloux days), Mrs. O'Driscoll and I sat under her two row-anwood trees and watched a monarch butterfly chase Nerves around the yard. As soon as Nerves got settled down again and curled up for a snooze, the monarch was back right at his nose and Nerves was on his feet showing his teeth and being pretty ferocious. Then the monarch went out and came in again, this time not fluttering and playing but gliding and diving straight for Nerves, and Nerves took off across the sideroad until he realized he was heading right for the potato field and 10,000 potato bugs. He screeched to a stop and made a quick right and headed down towards the ice house and Mushrat Creek, and we waited for the splash.

I went again to the covered bridge to wait for Oscar to come by in his coupe. Lately I had gone part way with him. We even talked together a couple of times. He always seemed to be going to say something but he'd never say it.

If he didn't have stuff piled in the rumble seat I could sometimes ride back there. You felt like a king riding back there. Riding through your kingdom. Waving at the farmers along the road. The breeze flapping your shirt. You reach up sometimes, try to slap the leaves. You see a red-winged blackbird showing off his dive. You try to catch a handful of chokecherries when Oscar is rounding a curve close to the edge. Your hand is purple and sticky from the chokecherry juice. You watch the groundhogs praying in the fields, sitting up straight, just like in Foolish Father Foley's church. You are blinking at the sun flashing through the trees, following you along. Listening to the crows complaining about nothing. Smelling the sweetgrass and the clover. Hearing the heat bugs.

The King of Mushrat Creek.

Until you stop. Then the dust swirls up around you and you'd better hold your breath for a minute.

The trouble with riding outside like that though was that I wouldn't be able to talk to Oscar, find out more about his life, about his dead lover Ophelia, about what happened.

Ophelia dead.

Sometimes I walked down to Brennan's Hill for a small can of white paint maybe to touch up our milk separator shack. Past Old Mickey Malarkey's house, the road was lined with chokecherry trees and plum. Some of the plums were ripe enough to eat but were a bit hard, but the chokecherries were soft and juicy. Trouble was they turned your mouth purple and made you feel after like you just ate a cardboard box. I timed it so I would get to the General Store in Brennan's Hill at half past five. That gave me time to get the paint, talk for a while (this is where I learned to tell the different evergreen trees apart), and then walk over to meet the train from Ottawa at ten to six.

I stood beside Oscar McCracken's mail car and watched the train. The whistle echoed all over the valley between the hills and then the train rounded the curve out of the trees and roared and coughed and chuckled and burped and farted and screeched and stopped.

And the steam floating across the platform there tasted like metal.

Some people got off.

Nobody I knew, though.

One cloux day, Nerves and I strolled over to see if Old Mac Gleason had any news. It was fun watching Nerves try to stroll.

Old Mac sucked on his pipe for a while.

Then Nerves and Old Mac started a long staring contest.

Nerves often did this to people. Especially strangers. I never saw him lose one of those staring matches. I think that Nerves, in his other life, must have been a hypnotist. Old Mac looked away finally and Nerves lay down for a little snooze.

"And how's little Nerves today? You're looking well, Nerves. Keeping busy, are you?" Old Mac didn't like Nerves. Too much competition.

Nerves opened one eye. Then he wagged one ear as if to say, "I'm fine, Old Mac Gleason. And how are *you* this fine morning? How's your verandah doing? Do you think we'll get some rain? What do you hear about the new bridge? Are you in favour of tearing down the old one or leaving it there for posterity? Do you think the devil will get you for not going to church? Does living beside a graveyard bother you at night? Do you know everybody's business in Mushrat Creek? Do you think you'll go to hell for making fun of Father Foley? Is your pipe empty again? Is that why it makes that sucking noise? When you spit off the verandah, do you always spit in the same place? Or do you wait to see which way the wind is blowing?

82

When you were young, did you ever cry? Did anybody ever say, 'be a man'? Does your rocking chair squeak the same way each time? When it was new, did it squeak? Did you ever write a letter to a girl when you didn't know her address?"

Nerves could say quite a bit with a little wag of his ear.

Cloux days came in handy.

I went for a walk up the road and talked for a minute to Mrs. Brown over the fence.

She was in her hollyhocks.

You could hardly see her.

You could hardly hear her.

She was Ophelia Brown's mother.

In my letter I tried to explain to F^3 about Ophelia's mother, Mrs. Brown.

I said in the letter that Mrs. Brown looked like a cup and saucer that you only used on Sunday. Then I said she looked like meringue on the top of a lemon pie. That sounded even more silly than the cup and saucer one. But I left them both in anyway. Then I tried to say that Mrs. Brown looked like a little glass statue of a ballet dancer. I liked the sound of that one so I left that in, too.

Later on I decided to try that she looked like a ripe milkweed pod. And, like ripe milkweed in a wind, if you blew on her, she'd come all apart and float away. And there'd be monarch butterflies all around you.

I smiled at Nerves while I thought about F^3 reading this letter (if I ever found her address), and what a picture she would have of Ophelia Brown's mother: a cup and saucer, lemon pie, glass ballet dancer, milkweed with monarchs.

Then I told her in the letter how sad it was about Oscar and his dead lover Ophelia Brown, and I even tried to talk about F³ and me and about our love affair and how we were apart, sort of like Ophelia and Oscar. I knew I was getting a little too dramatic but I couldn't help it. Then I said our love affair was sort of like two potato bugs, one on one leaf at one end of the potato field and the other on a potato plant leaf way down at the other end of the field. I knew how dumb it all sounded so I read the whole thing out to Nerves. When I got to the part about the potato bugs, Nerves ran into the kitchen and hid behind the stove.

Then I wrote that F³ and I were like fire and wood. She was the fire and I was the wood and the flames were our love and the sparks were the love words we said to each other and the smoke was the fights we had. Then I wrote that *she* was the wood and *I* was the fire and that the heat from the flames was the ache in my heart and the ashes were the rest of the cruel world when we were apart and by this time I was so mixed up that I tried to change it all to where she was a squirrel and I was a nut.

But I didn't say in the letter what was on my mind all the time. About the bridge. And about Oscar McCracken.

And if they tore down the bridge, what would he do. Poor Oscar. If we could only help him!

But O'Driscoll had his petition ready.

Maybe something was going to happen.

TREE GROWS OUT OF
BOY'S NOSE!

Everybody was talking and arguing about the covered bridge. Some wanted to keep it. Some wanted to tear it down. Some thought Prootoo was going to get a lot of profit from the contract for ripping it down. Some said maybe they should burn it down. Have a big corn roast!

Some didn't care. A job is a job.

Some wanted to leave it there for future generations. For Posterity.

"Future generations?" said the biggest farmer of them all. "What would you want to do that for? I suppose if you built a new barn, you'd leave the old barn there, all falling down and rotten so's future generations could stand around and admire it and say, My, look at the tumbled-down old shack they used for a barn in those days! I wonder why they bothered leavin' that there at all. Sure, it's only an eyesore!"

On our noon hour, one farmer, while he was eating a pig's leg for his dinner, gave us a little speech about the history of the bridge.

"Imagine them building our covered bridge in 1900! Everybody from all over the countryside coming with their picks and shovels and tools to work on the bridge. Just like building a barn! The walls, put up one big piece at a time, just like a barn, and the roof beam and the rafters and then lumber and the shingles—just like a barn and the hammers all hammering and the saws all sawing away and the men all shouting and then the big outdoor picnic at the church and the pies and cakes and beans and potatoes and bread and pork and tea and onions and cabbage and pickles and even tomatoes if it was the fall! Oh, it must have been lovely!

"And not one car came through the new covered bridge for a long long time. Only sleighs and wagons and carts!

"Will it fit a load of hay? Will it take a load of logs?

"Then it's all right!

"And after that, only a few cars a year came. And maybe a truck. Then a few more cars and trucks. And then more. And more.

"And then, in the last few years, it seemed like every day there was more cars and bigger trucks.

"So now we need a new bridge.

"Time to tear down the old bridge and build this nice new one like we're doing right now ... it's progress!"

It was quite a speech. Specially while you're eating a pig's leg.

Then Mickey Malarkey tried to tell a story about a cousin of his who was told not to shove a bean in his nose and did. And how the bean took root and began to grow and how the leaves were hanging out of his nostrils. Mickey tried to say they had to get hedge-clippers to trim some of the foliage hanging out of his nose, so they could get at the root and dig it out—and did he ever learn a lesson about shovin' things up your nose, especially beans!

But even Old Mickey Malarkey couldn't keep the subject off the bridge for long.

Sometimes some people who lived in cottages up the river in Beer Bay and on Beer Point would drive up and get out of their cars and ask about the bridge.

"Are they going to tear down the old covered bridge?" they'd say.

Then the argument would start all over again.

And the farmers that came from up in around Low would always seem to wind up arguing with the farmers from down in around Brennan's Hill.

And even though they might both be on the same side of the argument, they'd argue anyway.

Then somebody started up about how hard it is to keep *up* a covered bridge! All the things that can happen to it. Trucks hitting it. Heavy loads. Porcupines. Bark beetles. Lichen. Moss. Wind. Rain. Ants. People carving initials. Kids. Drunks. Vandals. Suicides.

And then some other people would start talking about the good stuff about the covered bridge, about how school kids could meet there to wait for the sleigh to take them to school in the winter except there were no more sleighs. And also about in the summer how kids could swing on a rope attached to a lower cord or stringer under the bridge and flip into the creek to swim and cool off; or how a farmer could rest his horses in there, stay in the bridge for a while to cool off and get their breath before they went up the other side pulling their load of hay or logs; or the advertisements you could pin up inside the wooden portals about meetings or dances; or how you could hold your breath and make a wish while you're passing through; or how at night your girl would be afraid (she was only pretending) because of the dark and you put your arm around her; and how trout would sometimes leap right out of Mushrat Creek and fall through the windows into the bridge!

And how magic it was when the bridge creaked in the wind.

And how lovers could meet in there.

And the drumming of the hooves, and the rumble of the wheels.

And then some other people would spoil it and tell how a farmer once hanged himself in the bridge because his crops wouldn't grow. Was it true? Maybe. Maybe not. Maybe it was another covered bridge. What difference did it make?

And then everybody started thinking of Oscar McCracken, but nobody mentioned him. And Ophelia Brown. And nobody said her name, either.

On Friday of the week when the news came out that they were going to tear down the old covered bridge as soon as one lane of the new bridge was finished, O'Driscoll was ready.

The night before, I told Mrs. O'Driscoll and him about how Oscar would talk four times a day to his dead lover, Ophelia Brown.

"We have to save this bridge," said O'Driscoll. "Not only for Oscar, but for Posterity. In my travels I have learned that without a past, we have no future!"

Mrs. O'Driscoll rolled her eyes. "What a Romantic," she said.

"You'll get fired," I said.

"No, I won't," he said. "I'm on the side of right! The side of History!"

O'Driscoll had a plan.

Everbody knew that on Friday, about half past

one, Prootoo would go to Wakefield to get the money for our pay. The bank closed at three o'clock so she always left in the truck with her husband who loved her, Ovide, to drive down to Wakefield and get the money before the bank closed.

At 1:30, O'Driscoll started taking the petition around to the bridge workers asking them to sign if they were in favour of saving the covered bridge.

I was watching him.

The first person he talked to was the biggest farmer of them all, who was a pretty good mechanic and who was lying under the generator, working on it.

O'Driscoll lay there under the generator with him. Their legs, sticking out, were the very same.

They had on the same overalls and the same boots. Almost everybody wore the same-coloured overalls. Everybody bought them at the same store. There was only one kind.

The generator was right beside Prootoo's shack.

But the truck was gone. Everything was O.K. She wouldn't be back for quite a while.

We were sure Prootoo was gone in the truck to Wakefield to get the pay.

Suddenly the door of the shack opened and Prootoo stood there listening to O'Driscoll talking to the mechanic about signing the petition about saving the bridge. You could hear him explaining it.

You could tell that she didn't know *who* it was under there, but she could hear *what* it was he was saying.

She had a can of white paint in her hands. She began to lean away over to look under the generator to see who was talking about this petition about the bridge.

Some of us were watching.

We knew that if she got down on her hands and knees and looked under she would find out it was O'Driscoll doing the talking and fire him on the spot for trying to start a strike.

Just then Mr. Proulx's truck drove up in a cloud of dust. He said in French to her that they had to go. Right now! They were in a hurry! Wakefield. The bank closes at three! Tout d'suite!

Prootoo then got a very wise and crafty look on her face.

She didn't say a word to her husband as he gave her a little kiss on the cheek out the truck window. While he kissed her, she never took her eyes off O'Driscoll's pants. Then, as she walked around the front of the truck to get in, she deliberately spilled some white paint on the right leg of O'Driscoll's overalls.

Then she put the can of paint in the shack, got in the truck, and they took off.

O'Driscoll, on his back, worked his way out from under the generator.

"Thank you, Paddy," said O'Driscoll. "That's good enough for me."

"Did he sign his name?" I said.

"No, he didn't," said O'Driscoll, "but he said he liked the idea of going around and asking people. He said he thought that was fair."

I told O'Driscoll about what Prootoo did. The paint on the pants.

"I heard the truck taking off," said O'Driscoll as he looked at the right pant leg of his overalls. "Why do you think she did this?"

And then I thought. Then the more I thought, the more excited I got. I had a funny feeling that I was going to know the answer. The answer was right around the corner! Any minute now! Don't think

90

too hard. It might go away. Why did she do that? She didn't know who it was. She didn't know who was saying these things about the bridge because all the legs of all the overalls looked the same.

But she put on the paint. On the pants.

This is payday!

Tonight at six, we line up.

For our pay.

All our pants will be together!

She'll pick the pants with the paint!

"That's it!" I said to O'Driscoll.

"What's it?" said O'Driscoll.

"Tonight. At six o'clock! In the pay line-up! She'll check the pants. She'll make a speech. She'll fire you! Just like teachers do in school sometimes. Make an example of you ... fire you in front of everybody. That's what she's like!"

Before I was finished, O'Driscoll was looking in the supply shack.

I thought he was looking for paint remover.

But no. He came out with Prootoo's can of white paint.

"An old trick I learned in the navy," he said.

"What are you going to do?" I said.

"Follow me," said O'Driscoll as he took a quick look over his shoulder. "Follow me!"

WOMAN'S FACE SPROUTS
PINE KNOTS!

I tried to explain in my letter to Fleurette the look on Prootoo's face when she came out of the shack at six o'clock and saw all the farmers lined up so straight, just like in school.

Every farmer had a splotch of white paint on the right leg of his overalls.

What a coincidence! Which worker was passing around the petition?

Who knows!

Prootoo's face was like a crowbar, I said in Fleurette's letter. No, it was more like a bag of cement. No, it was like a one-by-six piece of pine lumber with too many knots, and full of bent nails.

It was like a flying sledge hammer.

It was fun writing it. But I didn't admit that I felt kind of bad. I felt a little sorry for Prootoo. She wasn't as bad as they thought. In fact, sometimes she was almost nice. Maybe it was because I knew she liked me. I don't know.

The farmers on the bridge had so much fun that day that they all signed the petition whether they agreed with it or not.

It said this:

"I, the undersigned, refuse to tear down the covered bridge.

I would rather save it for Posterity. For, without a past, we have no future."

Saturday at noon, while she was ringing the time-to-quit bell, Prootoo had the petition put in her hand by O'Driscoll himself.

GRAVEYARD FENCE
MOVES DURING NIGHT!

The next day was Sunday, and it was a day that the people of Mushrat Creek would never forget.

Father Foley started in on his usual sermon and was scaring himself half to death about Hell. Then he paused and changed the subject a bit. He started talking about Obedience. About following the rules about doing as you're told. About how Satan was cast out of Heaven because of Pride and about how Adam and Eve, especially Eve, were kicked out of the Garden of Eden because they wouldn't do as they were told and how the Lord once sent a big flood to drown all the people who wouldn't do as they were told which was just about everybody and the way Father Foley told it, it looked like God could hardly get *anybody* to do what they were told.

Then Father Foley whipped out a long sheet of paper.

It was O'Driscoll's petition!

"It has come to my attention," shouted Father Foley, "that the workers who are working on our spanking new bridge are refusing to honour part of their contract. Their *Duty*. This, my parishioners, is a disgrace to this fine community. Mr. Proulx is a fine businessman and an excellent craftsman. He has been hired and is being paid by the provincial and local authorities to do his duty. He will do his duty. And you will do yours! As God is my witness, the covered bridge will be torn down when the time comes for it to be torn down! And this foolish petition is now null and void!"

Father Foley then tore the petition four or five times and threw it down at his feet in the pulpit.

The way Father Foley told it, it sounded sort of like God wanted the farmers to tear down their own bridge that their fathers had built.

Everybody was shocked.

But not as shocked as they were a few seconds later when a voice came from the back of the church.

"That bridge is none of your damn business, Father Foley!" the voice shouted.

Everybody turned around.

It was Oscar McCracken doing the shouting. Quiet Oscar McCracken was almost screaming in Father Foley's church!

"What happens to the covered bridge is none of your damned business, Father Foley!" Oscar was choking and crying.

Oscar McCracken, who never said boo to anybody, was yelling and *swearing* at Father Foley in Father Foley's church!

"I wish you were *dead*, Father Foley! I wish you were dead and burning in Hell!" screamed Oscar McCracken and ran out the open doors, knocking over the pile of collection baskets on the table there.

When I looked back up at Father Foley, everybody was looking down. Not looking at anything.

Ashamed of Oscar McCracken.

Afraid of Father Foley's rage.

For the rest of the service, nobody would look at Father Foley. Everybody looked down at their feet.

When we left, Father Foley wasn't at the door to wish us goodbye.

That evening, under the rowanwood trees, we were quiet. There wasn't much to say. Nobody spoke to anybody, it seemed, since Oscar stood up and swore at the priest in church that morning. People moved out of the church quietly, not speaking much of anything to anybody. Some of the mothers maybe told their kids to hush up or hurry up or don't do that, but that was about all anybody said.

And we were sad. Sad for Oscar and Oscar's family. Because now, for a while anyway, nobody was going to talk too much to Oscar, even though they liked him and everything. Now, when he'd deliver the mail and maybe they would be out at their mailboxes, they would maybe say good afternoon and then look down at their mail right away so as not to look into Oscar's shame in his eyes.

And we were worried. Now that the bridge was going to be torn down for sure, maybe everybody in Mushrat Creek would say to us, I told you so, I told you that old relic would be nothing but trouble, and maybe people would think we were strangers, poking into their business, especially O'Driscoll with his petition. Maybe they'd start to say he tricked them into signing it and that now they were in trouble because Father Foley saw every one of those names on the list and knew every one of them and had visited every one of them when they were sick and when their kids were sick or the old folks were dying and Father Foley prayed for all of them and loved them and now they turn around and do something like this? Be Disobedient? And maybe they'd say it was all because of those new people, the what-do-you-call-em's, the O'Driscolls.

I tried to change the subject, maybe get O'Driscoll talking.

I asked him a question.

"What did you mean when you said you learned that trick about the paint on the pants in the navy?"

"Oh, that," said O'Driscoll, taking a quick look behind him at Nerves, who was walking by with one of our hens. "That was the way you could come in late at night, a way after you were supposed to, past curfew, run right past the Duty Officer, you roar right down into the mess where your hammock is already slung, give all the full hammocks a swing as you go by, then get into yours without even taking your clothes off. A few seconds later when the Duty Officer sticks his head in the hatch to get your number, *all* the hammocks are swinging! Get it? Who just came in late and got in their hammock? Just about everybody, sir!"

It was something but not the real O'Driscoll.

Mrs. O'Driscoll sighed.

The bridge would be gone. Nothing would be the same. Maybe we'd have to move again.

Hopeless.

Nerves was back from walking the hen to the henhouse and was sniffing some plants alongside the house.

I tried O'Driscoll again.

"What are those plants Nerves is so interested in over there?"

I knew that if O'Driscoll didn't know the answer he would make something up.

I hoped he didn't know the answer.

"Those plants? You didn't pull one up, did you? Because if you pull one up by hand, all alone, you'll die a horrible death by strangulation within the next twenty-four hours. Why would you want to pull one up? I'll tell you why."

You could tell O'Driscoll was glad to talk about something that would take his mind off his torn-up petition.

Mrs. O'Driscoll eased back in her chair to get comfortable. She was going to try to enjoy this one.

"Did you learn this in your travels?" she said and shut her eyes like she always did when she didn't expect an answer.

"They're called mandrake plants. People take the mandrake root and grind it up and make a powder and mix it with pig's blood and drink it. It can make a woman have as many babies as she wants and a little touch of it once and a while can make a man very handsome indeed. But too much of it has been known to drive a lad right around the corner and out of his mind. Julian, one of the emperors of the Roman Empire, took so much of it that he thought for a while he was turned into a goat and nearly died after he ate most of his blanket one night."

Mrs. O'Driscoll sighed.

"How do you pull it up without getting strangled within twenty-four hours?" O'Driscoll went on. "I'm glad you asked that, Hubbo me boy. You *don't* pull it up. You get a small rope, tie one end of it to the base of the stem of the mandrake and tie the other end of the rope around the neck of a *dog*."

I looked down at Nerves, who was studying some ants in the sweetgrass.

He glanced up at us with a sarcastic look on his face.

"Then," said O'Driscoll, "you *chase* the dog!"

"Where did you say you learned all this, again?"

said Mrs. O'Driscoll, trying to trap O'Driscoll. She kept her eyes closed this time, which meant she knew she wasn't going to get an answer and that she didn't really want one anyway.

"And when the mandrake is uprooted, you'll notice two remarkable things," O'Driscoll kept on. "One: you hear a small, blood-curdling scream. Two: you'll see that the root is shaped exactly like a little statue of a man!"

I was right. O'Driscoll didn't know what those plants were at all.

After dark, Nerves and I went out to trim the lamps on the covered bridge. The moonlight sparkled on the water of Mushrat Creek and pierced through the openings of the bridge, sending bars of softness onto the carriageway inside.

The moonlight turned the red side of the bridge into silver.

It was sad to think that the covered bridge would soon be gone forever.

After the lamps, Nerves and I took a walk. Behind the church in the sexton's cottage there was a light shining out the curtained window.

The door was open a bit. I politely opened it some more.

"Oscar?"

Oscar, sitting at the table, with his sad eyes.

"I can't go home. My family won't talk to me. I'll stay here tonight or with Mrs. Brown. Hello, Nerves. How are you tonight?"

Nerves sat with his head up and his paws together. Best behaviour. He liked Oscar McCracken. He liked riding in the rumble seat of Oscar McCracken's coupe car.

"I shouldn't have spoke like that in church. I shouldn't have shouted them things."

Oscar let out a long, long sigh.

"Everything's over," he said.

Then he looked at Nerves a while and smiled a little bit.

"I met you before you met me, you know," he said, leaning over to Nerves.

Nerves, sitting even straighter.

Oscar turned to me.

"You know, Hubbo, I never did in all my born days ever see a dog faint, so help me God, until that night."

My mouth must have fallen open, because there was a moth trying to fly into it.

"You?" I said. "That night?"

"Come out, I'll show you."

In the goat pen, on a little clothesline, hung a long white dress and a blue hat with a wide brim.

"I did it to try and make Father Foley move Ophelia's grave inside the graveyard fence. It was the second stupidest thing I ever did. This morning in church was the stupidest. Now she'll never get in."

"That was you?"

"That was me. I thought I'd meet Father Foley coming back from visiting the sick. Turned out it was you."

"I should have known it was no ghost," I said.

"Why?" said Oscar.

"The splash!" I said. "Ghosts don't splash when they hit the water. A big splash!"

"I know." Oscar was almost laughing. "I did a belly flop. Stupid me!"

Then we both laughed.

And then we stood for a while until the goat poked her head out of her little barn.

Nerves got around behind my legs.

"I'm goin' to leave this place forever," Oscar said

quietly. "But there's one thing I got to do before I go. And that thing I got to do, I got to do tonight."

Oscar went into the sexton's cottage.

There was clanging and rattling around in there.

Oscar came out with a roll of page wire. And a post-hole digger. And a shovel. He had wire-cutters and a carpenter's belt full of tools and nails.

"Do you want to give me a hand?" he said.

Up in the graveyard Oscar already had a cedar post cut and hidden in the long grass a little away from Ophelia Brown's grave.

He was all ready. He knew exactly what to do. He had been thinking about it for years.

Ophelia's grave was just outside the fence right between two fence posts.

The first thing he did was cut the page wire away from the two posts and leave an open gateway in the fence.

Then we dug a hole on the other side of Ophelia Brown's grave and we sank the post and tamped it down with rocks and earth. This was a strong post.

Then we cinched the new page wire to the first original post, brought it out around the new post and stapled it there, then brought it back to the second original post.

We cleaned up around the job and walked back a bit to look.

The grave of Ophelia Brown, Oscar McCracken's lover, was now inside the graveyard fence.

In fact, it looked kind of special.

It looked like the fence went along and then said, whoops, let's jog out here a bit, we don't want to forget to include our Ophelia Brown, now do we?

Back at the sexton's cottage we sat on the grass and drank cold water. Nerves seemed glad to get out of the graveyard.

Oscar was calm now, and in a sort of a good mood.

"Maybe I'll wait a few days before I leave. See what happens. I'm not mad at Father Foley. It's not his fault. It's the rules."

Then, Oscar, just for a joke, pulled the wide-brimmed hat off the line and put it carefully over the goat's horns.

"This looks good on you, do you know that?"

We both laughed. The goat bleated.

Even Nerves looked at the goat without hiding because she looked so harmless in that hat that she wouldn't hurt a fly.

Oscar said he was tired and went in. I noticed he didn't shut the goat pen gate, but I was too tired to care. He could do it later when he went up to Mrs. Brown's to sleep.

Nerves and I went home.

I fell onto my straw mattress, mud and all. And I drifted and rode off into a sleep.

There was a big dance in the covered bridge.

I was dancing with the biggest farmer of them all. Fleurette was there, dancing with Father Foley. She was wearing a white dress with lace, blue shoes and a blue hat with a broad brim. She had a white rag tying up her black hair. Some of the farmers were tearing down the bridge during the dance. There was hammering, with the sound of little hammers like the hoofbeats of a goat. Oscar was up in the rafters trying to hang himself and underneath us Mushrat Creek was boiling, spurting red-hot lava. O'Driscoll came riding through the bridge on a dol-phin while Mrs. O'Driscoll, floating, played the fid-dle, her face the face of an angel.

Then the music gets faster and Old Mac Gleason has got Nerves and he's throwing him out the wind-vent and Mushrat Creek is full, like in the spring, but it's not water that fills the creek and lashes against the sides of the bridge, it's potato bugs! And Ophelia Brown is trying to stop Old Mac Gleason and my feet are nailed to the deck and I can't move! I've got my nail puller but I can't move! No...! No...! No...!

"Hubbo! Hubbo me boy! Wake up, lad! It's me, O'Driscoll. Get up. Get up. Quick!"

It was. It was O'Driscoll, shaking me awake.

"Come quick, boy! Something terrible has happened! It's Father Foley! They found him in the bridge! He's dead! They say somebody must have killed him. Get your pants on!"

MAN'S HEAD TURNS
INTO PUMPKIN!

Everybody working on the new bridge was saying that Father Foley didn't just die, he was murdered. They weren't saying it very loud, mind you. Maybe only whispering it, or saying it without saying it at all.

For instance, you wouldn't actually hear somebody come right out and say, "I think so-and-so murdered Foolish Father Foley last night in the covered bridge." Oh, no, you wouldn't hear that. But you might hear somebody say this: "They say that there's rumours going around that some people have heard others say that they've been told that there's a suspicion that something bad that you wouldn't like to say out loud happened to Father Foley in the covered bridge last night."

And the other person would maybe say, "Well, he died in there, we all know *that* for sure."

And the first person might say, "Yes, we do know that for sure, but they say that maybe they know *how* or why he died."

And the other person would say, "Well, what *is* it that they say is what maybe happened?"

And then the person who started it all would probably say, "Oh, I wouldn't like to say."

And then some other people would stop working on the new bridge and put down a hammer and lean on a shovel and then start talking about who it was who maybe *killed* Foolish Father Foley from Farrelton in the covered bridge last night.

One might say, while he was leaning on his shovel, "They say that people have heard people say that somebody, who maybe even some of us *know*, might be the one to be the *cause* of Father Foley's death."

And the other, while he was putting down his hammer, "Yes, and they say, now don't get me wrong, I'm not saying this but they say that *that* person who was maybe *in* on the Father's horrible death the other night in the covered bridge was somebody we know that has something to do with delivering the mail around here in this part of the country."

We all carried steel rods for about three hours.

Before noon two policemen drove up with Oscar and Mrs. Brown in the back.

The policeman asking the questions had a big wart on his nose.

"This is the young gentleman here," said Mrs. Brown, showing me to the policeman. You could hardly hear Mrs. Brown.

The policeman with the wart on his nose was very quiet and polite and friendly. He asked where I was last night, what was I doing, what time was it, when did I last see Oscar?

I told him.

"And this graveyard business. What were you doing there?"

"We were fixing the fence."

The policeman's wart seemed to swell up a bit.

He got back in the car and they drove quietly away.

We carried steel rods until noon.

I was so tired I could hardly talk.

Lunch hour came at last.

"They're saying Oscar could have sneaked out of Mrs. Brown's after she was asleep and waited for Father Foley inside the bridge," O'Driscoll said. "And hit him over the head."

"I know," I said. "But it's not true. He couldn't have!"

"Pretty strange, all right, Hubbo me boy," O'Driscoll sighed. "Everybody heard Oscar threaten the Father. That's a very serious thing, Hubbo. Are you sure you didn't see Oscar do anything last night?"

Now O'Driscoll thought *I* was holding something back. That maybe *I* was a witness to something. I'd probably spend the rest of my life in jail.

Or be hanged by the neck until I was dead.

O'Driscoll all of a sudden gave me a hug.

He must have realized he made me feel bad.

"I'm sorry, Hubbo me boy. Listen now, don't worry. I know you're telling the truth, and when you tell the truth, everything always turns out fine!"

I wondered what Mrs. O'Driscoll would say if she heard O'Driscoll talk that way about the truth.

The rest of the hour we spent half listening to Mickey Malarkey telling us a pack of lies about his father and his ancestors.

It's hard to imagine, when your muscles are aching and your bones are sore and your eyes are full of dried sweat and your stomach is so full of food and tea that there's steam coming out of your mouth; it's hard to imagine somebody as old as Mickey Malarkey having a father.

He told us his father, Justin, *also* lived to be 114 years of age and had a head bigger than a large pumpkin. He said that his father Justin's great-*grandfather* whose name was Brendan and was born in the year 1695, the year before the discovery of *peppermint* also lived to be 114 years of age!

Later in the afternoon but long before quitting time, Prootoo rang her bell and when we all were around, Ovide Proulx made an announcement:

"Everybody will report to the church at five o'clock. The town council has got the coroner over dere from Wakefield because he wants to tell everybody personally what 'appened to da body of Poor Father Foley. Also, de police are dere too and dey want to question everybody about what dey can tell after dey hear what the coroner is going to tell. Work is finish for today."

Everybody was walking and packing up and asking questions and guessing what the coroner was going to say.

We headed up the road in small groups towards the church. It was going to seem funny being in there without Father Foley yelling about Hell.

The singing farmer sang part of his song behind us:

Brian O'Lynn and his wife and wife's mother
All went up to the church together
The church it was locked, and they couldn't get in
"We'll pray to the Devil," says Brian O'Lynn!

I ducked behind the church and took a look around the sexton's cottage.

The gate was open to the goat pen.

The dress hanging on the line was gone.

The goat was gone!

Could it be? Could that be what happened?

PRIEST'S BLOOD SUCKED
UP BY SPONGE!

News that the coroner was coming up from Wakefield spread fast, and when he arrived there was quite a crowd waiting for him in the church to hear what he had to say about Father Foley's death. Just about everybody was there. Even Oscar.

And beside him, the policeman with the wart.

Mrs. O'Driscoll slid in beside us in the pew we were in.

"Oscar's goat's gone!" I whispered to her.

"What do you mean?" she said.

"I think I know what happened," I said.

"Shh," she said.

"Ladies and gentlemen. The autopsy showed that Father Foley did not die of a blow to the head. That wound was superficial and probably was caused by his fall. Nor did he die of a heart attack or of a brain tumour or a blood clot or any other such normal causes of sudden death. No, the cause of death in this case is much more rare."

The coroner waited. He thought that everybody standing around would look at each other and say words like "rare" and "normal" and go "oooh" and "ahhh." But they didn't. They just sat there.

Then the coroner said some more.

"Father Foley died of a mysterious and sinister condition sometimes called Neurogenic Shock or Vasovagal Collapse. Vasovagal Collapse is due to a loss of peripheral arteriolar resistance resulting from reflex dilation in areas of skeletal muscle. The pooling of blood in peripheral vascular beds with loss of vascular tone results in inadequate venous return, a fall in cardiac output and subsequent reduction in arterial blood pressure. The heart has not sufficient fluid on which to contract. The lost blood of Father Foley did not pour out of him. It disappeared into his vastly dilated capillary bed and into his tissues.

"Something paralyzed the vast capillary bed of Father Foley's body, causing extreme dilation. His blood then disappeared into it as if sucked up by a sponge!" He waited again. He was waiting for people to start asking questions. They didn't. They just sat there.

"What could have paralyzed Father Foley's capillary bed, you ask? All he was doing was passing through the covered bridge." The coroner seemed mad. The audience was not co-operating.

"There is only one answer to that," said the coroner slowly. "And that answer is FEAR!

"FEAR!" he repeated. Nobody moved.

"Yes, my friends. I have to conclude that Father Foley dropped dead because someone, or something, scared him to death!"

Now the audience co-operated.

This made sense! Now everybody started talking at once.

Of course Father Foley could have been scared to death!

Didn't he almost scare himself to death just about every Sunday during his sermon about Hell?

What about when he just about jumped out of his skin the time the goat came into the church that time?

"He certainly was the *jumpiest* priest we've had around here for a while," said Old Mickey Malarkey.

They were all talking now.

"I knew it!" I said to myself.

I knew it.

GOAT POSSESSED
BY SATAN!

When the coroner was finished his report, the policeman and his wart took over and a discussion started.

I slipped out the small north door that Oscar always used. Nobody saw me.

I ran down the road, through the covered bridge, up our side road, under the red chandeliers of our rowanwood trees, around the house, past the woodpile and the summer kitchen, past the log stable and around by the manure pile and the pig pen, up through the pine bush and turned onto the old logging road towards the Gatineau River.

Beyond the corduroy there was a section of road where a purplish brown mat of dead pine needles stretched back as far as you could see into the bush.

This part of the road was damp clay and would show tracks.

I found what I thought I'd find.

Small cloven hoofprints!

I looked down the road. The evening light was slanting and filtering into the tunnel of tall sumac and poplar trees. The road turned and dipped into gloom.

I turned back and went home to wait.

I stuck my head in the big stone crock and pulled out a chunk of homemade bread.

O'Driscoll hit the door open and looked behind himself and said, "There's a lot of talk goin' about a missing goat Hubbo me boy. What's goin' on?"

"That's it!" I said. "That's what happened! I heard the hammering last night! I heard the hooves! I'm sure the goat got out! She ran through the bridge! Met Father Foley coming home from his rounds with the sick. The timing is perfect. I heard the goat hooves last night when I was half asleep! We left the gate open. The goat ate part of the dress off the line, got tangled up in it, ran out the gate and met Father Foley in the bridge. And she was wearing that hat! There's fresh tracks on the road. Let's go! The goat came down our road. I heard her!"

"Let's go and get the policeman to come with us," said O'Driscoll.

I guess everybody must have told the policeman with the wart on his nose what Father Foley was like because he seemed to enjoy the idea of coming with us to follow the goat tracks.

On our way, I explained to him about the hat and the dress and Oscar's ghost trick and the open gate.

"Quite a place, this Mushrat Creek," said the policeman with the wart. "Ghosts and goats and covered bridges and devils and dead priests."

His wart was starting to look kind of cute.

We were walking down the slope over the stink-horn fungus and edging our way down the bank.

And there she was. Tangled up in some branches. Looking pretty lost. She gave a little bleat to us.

The hat was still over her horns.

The dress tangled over her body so that running through a covered bridge towards you in the dark,

112

the dress flying and those eyes behind the hat brim and the thundering hooves could be pretty scary all right.

Specially if you were Father Foley with his light. Poor Father Foley!

MAN LAUGHS FOR
WHOLE WEEK!

Three weeks later, on one of my cloux days, I went up on Dizzy Peak to pick some blueberries. While I picked I spoke to Fleurette as though I was writing more of the letter. I tried to make it dramatic. I tried to make it sound like she was reading it.

From up here on Dizzy Peak you can see the whole world. To the east, the dam and the big flooded country above it and below it the narrow fast river the way it used to be when only the first Canadians lived here.

North there is the town of Low and then Venosta, and in the mist of the mountains, maybe, Farrelton.

West, rolling humpbacked mountains and lakes here and there like broken bits of mirrors.

And the covered bridge down there, with its new paint job.

And the new bridge just above it, a cement slab.

I could hear her voice reading it. And her sighing.

I already wrote in her letter how it was that the bridge didn't get torn down after all.

It was Mrs. O'Driscoll who figured it out. And Prootoo.

At a county council general meeting Mrs. O'Driscoll got Prootoo to get up and make a motion. Mrs. O'Driscoll told her to move that the covered bridge be dedicated as a monument to the late Father Foley. It was seconded by the biggest farmer of them all.

That way Ovide Proulx got the contract to paint the bridge instead of tearing it down.

How could anybody vote against that? Even Old Mac Gleason, who actually went to the meeting, had to put his hand up!

Business was business.

O'Driscoll laughed for almost a week about it until Mrs. O'Driscoll finally got sick of the whole story and shut him down by giving him the silence.

Now as Oscar McCracken travelled the bridge four times a day and paused each time inside, in the quiet there, he could, if he wanted to, read at each portal, a brass plaque.

The plaque said these words:

Let this covered bridge be dedicated to the memory of Father Francis Foley of Farrelton who gave his life herein for the people of his parish.
God Love Him
May He Rest Peacefully.

Up on Dizzy Peak, I pretended to write some more.

And here on Dizzy Peak, the sun beats on the rock and in between, the tough blueberry bushes growing in the moss, loaded with blueberries, powdered and fat, wait.

You lean over the edge, hanging by one hand to a ridge of rock a million years old and strip a handful of berries from a plant growing out of the side of the peak. Your pail on the ledge beside your hand is almost full, so you jam the handful of berries into your mouth instead.

The berries are hot and firm and sweet and you can feel them burst and pop in your mouth and the blue juice overflows down your chin.

You are eating the sun and the earth and the rain.

Fleurette would like that writing. If I could ever write it that way.

I got home with a pailful of blueberries, washed them and cleaned them, and put them on to simmer in some sugar for Mrs. O'Driscoll.

Later I met Oscar in the bridge, sat with him during his quiet time, and drove down with him to meet the train.

Sitting there on the fender of Oscar's car, my feet on the wooden station platform, my arms folded across my chest. I was feeling the muscles in my arms with my fingers. My muscles were hard and bulging from the work on the bridge.

My hands were rough and leathery from carrying the steel and the bags of cement. The fingers feeling my muscles that were strong and hard felt like steel hooks.

The train came howling around the bend in a cloud of soot and smoke and steam at exactly five to six and screamed and cried and moaned and chugged and grunted and sighed and farted and then stopped.

The bell was ringing and clanging and stabbing clean through the air and into the hills and up and down the track and off the station walls. The station master and his helper pulled a big red wagon by the tongue alongside the baggage car. I waited and watched Oscar sort his mail.

Some people were getting off the train carrying their bags and suitcases.

You could always tell when the last person was

off the train because the conductor would pick up the little step and put it back inside between the cars where he kept it.

I watched the conductor pick up the little step and get up into the train with it.

The train belched and started to move.

I looked over at Oscar.

He was wearing a big smile.

He had a letter in his hand.

He gave it to me, turned upside down.

I flipped it over and right away, the handwriting!

It was from Fleurette Featherstone Fitchell.